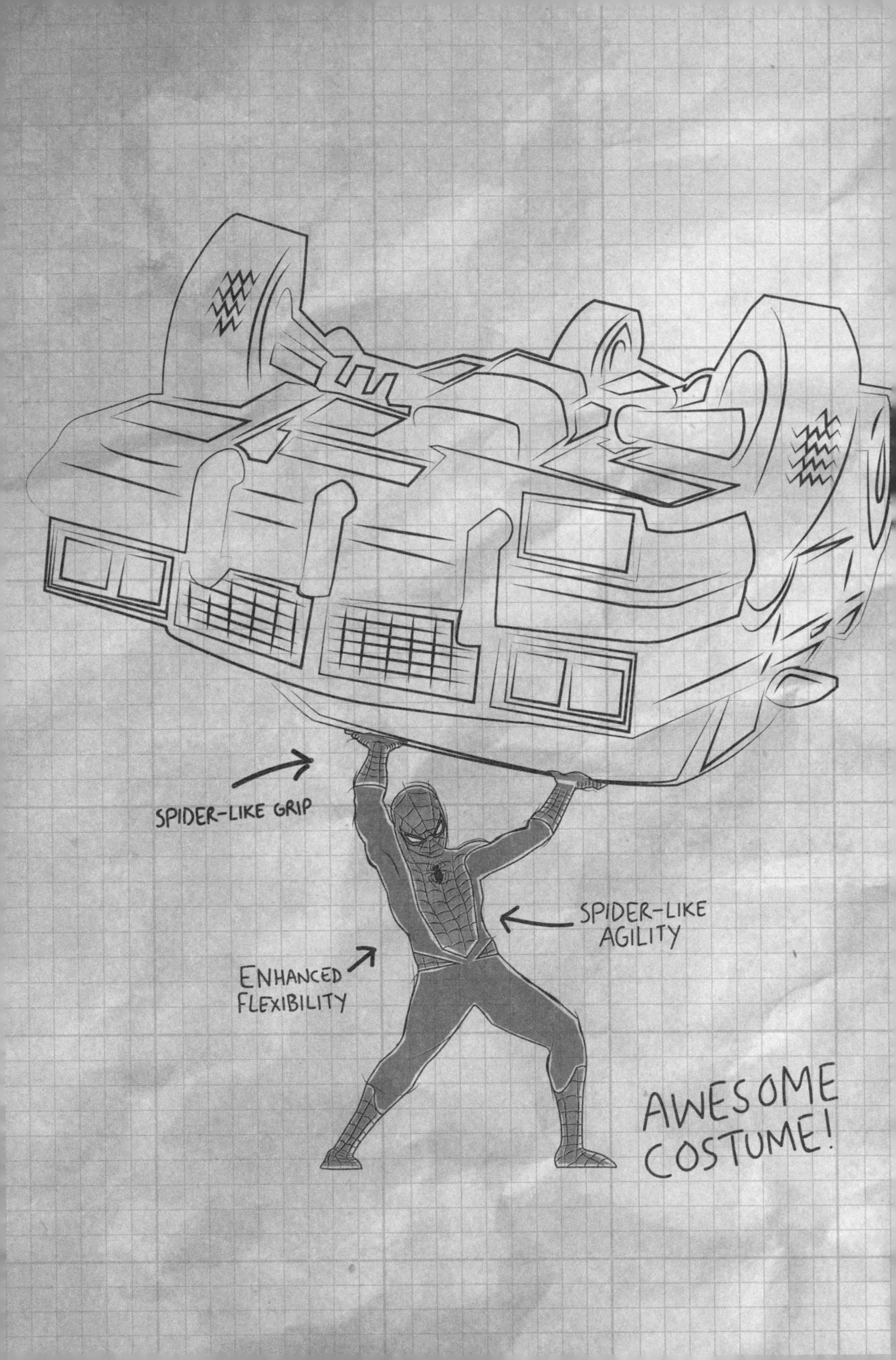
SPIDER-LIKE GRIP
SPIDER-LIKE AGILITY
ENHANCED FLEXIBILITY
AWESOME COSTUME!

MARVEL

SPIDER-MAN UNMASKED!

THE REAL JOURNAL OF PETER PARKER

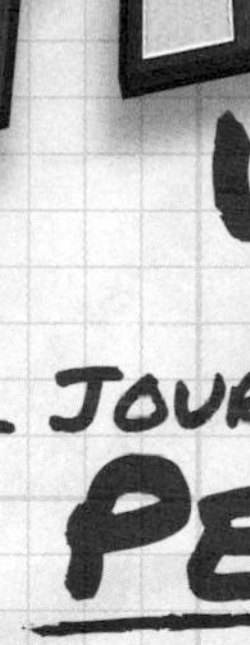

THAT'S ME!

SHHHHHH!!!

IT'S A SECRET, THOUGH!

studio fun INTERNATIONAL

I've been in the super hero business for quite some time now, but it's still hard to believe that I, Peter Parker, am actually the web-spinning, wall-crawling, amazing adventurer known as...

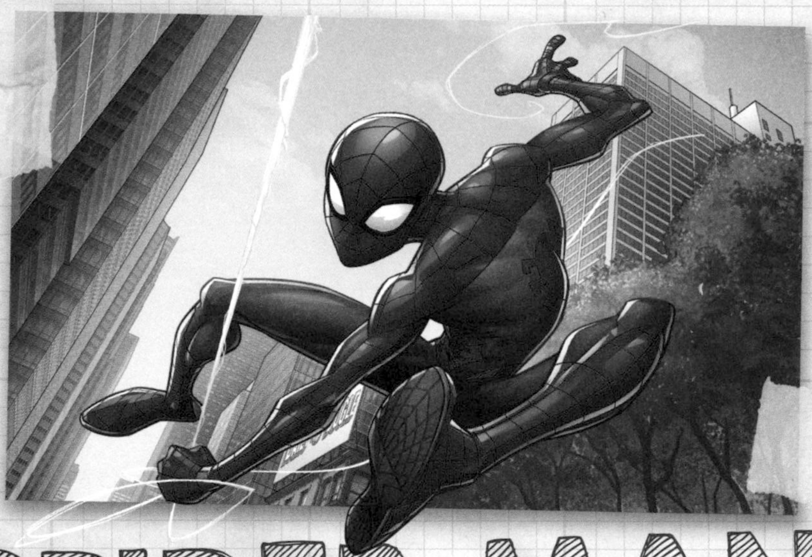

SPIDER-MAN!

We all know every super hero has a story to tell. Luckily, I have many stories to tell!

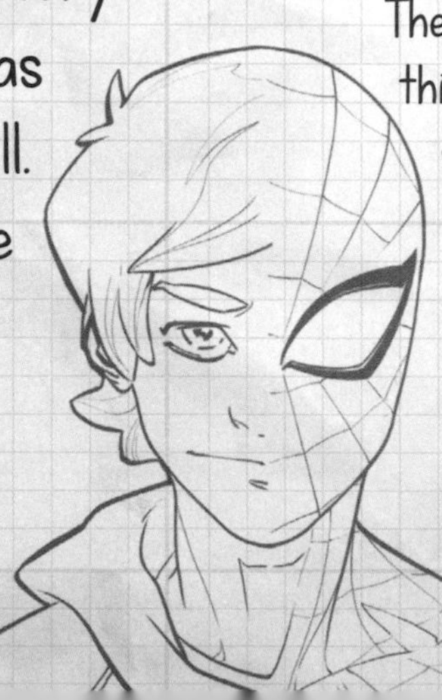

They've been collected here in this personal, private, top-secret journal...starting with **my very own super hero origin story** that I wrote the day it all began. Buckle up, kids.

It's a wild ride!

JOURNAL ENTRY 1:

There are no words to describe the day I had today.

AMAZING! SENSATIONAL!
SPECTACULAR!

Okay, so maybe there are a few words...but I'm pretty much still in shock. Maybe if I write things down I might be able to make sense of them and prove to myself that my imagination is **NOT** in hyper-drive.

It all started as a pretty typical day for "super nerd" Peter Parker (that's me!) at Midtown High. My homework was on point. I aced my Chemistry test. And I was the subject, yet again, of one of Flash Thompson's "public service announcements." How thoughtful. Even more thoughtful was having one of his lackeys snap a pic so he could post it all over social media.

See Exhibit A:

HEY, PUNY PARKER, YOU DROPPED YOUR BOOKS!

Aside from being made the laughingstock of first period, I did have another reason to go to school this morning: a field trip to The New York City Science Hall—the biggest location of the biggest brains in the Big Apple! World-famous Dr. Lori Froeb, a brilliant scientist, would show us the state-of-the-art high-tech labs and equipment being used in their research.

I packed all my photography gear to document every millisecond of the trip. Nothing was going to slip past my eye. This was going to be life-changing!

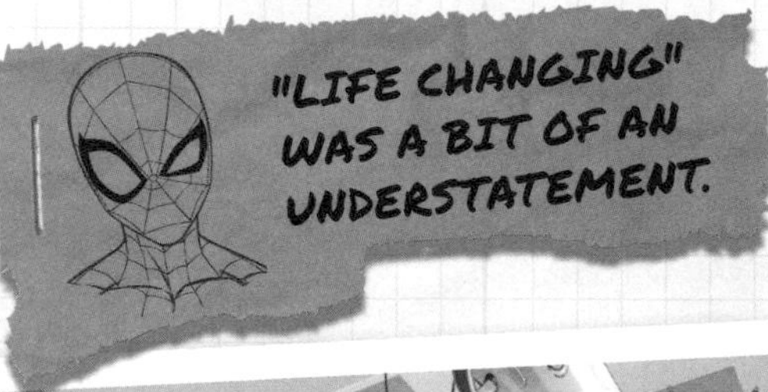
"LIFE CHANGING" WAS A BIT OF AN UNDERSTATEMENT.

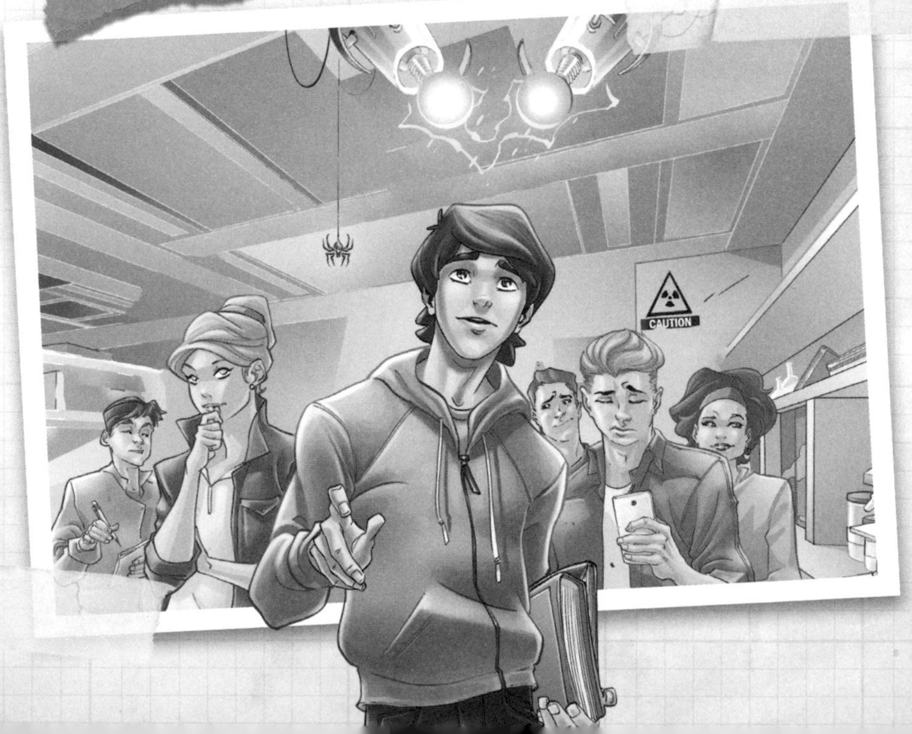
CAUTION

Upon entering the Science Hall, I had a major geek-out just standing in the lobby alone. The walls were lined with glass cases housing vintage microscopes, Geiger counters, astrolabes, and more.

Dr. Froeb brought us into the radioactive material research lab. As she explained her study of radiography in medical and healing arts, an itsy bitsy spider climbed right into the oncoming path of the radiation machine. Then that itsy bitsy radioactive spider bit me. **YEOWCH!**

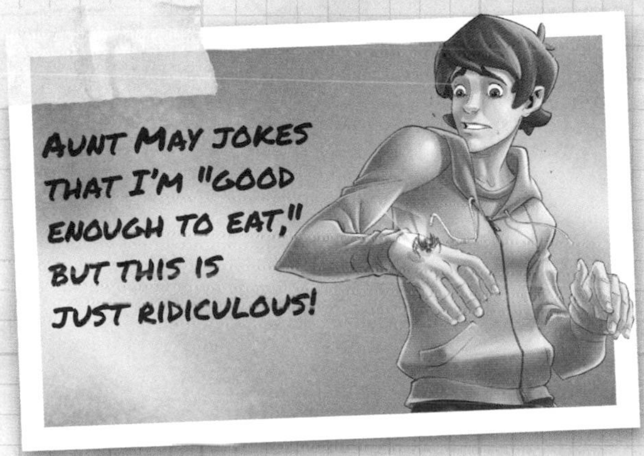
AUNT MAY JOKES THAT I'M "GOOD ENOUGH TO EAT," BUT THIS IS JUST RIDICULOUS!

SPIDER FACTS

- All spiders have eight legs. They are arthropods, like crabs and scorpions.
- Spider silk is possibly the strongest material in the world. Scientists believe that a strand of silk is much stronger than a strand of steel the same size.
- Arachnophobia is the fear of spiders.

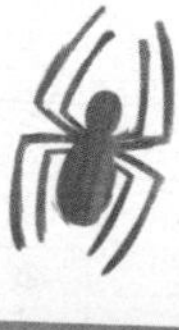

Journal Entry 2:

Yesterday was probably a dream, right? WRONG. I know there's the old saying "waking up on the wrong side of the bed," but I happened to wake up several feet above the bed... on the ceiling. **THE CEILING!!**

What was going on??? The only logical explanation I could come up with had to do with that radioactive spider bite. I started to BUG OUT big time. What if Aunt May or Uncle Ben walked in and saw me? How would I explain something I didn't understand myself?

Well, I could always say I was just hanging around.

Seriously, though. Am I turning into a SPIDER?

LIST OF "SYMPTOMS"

- SUPERHUMAN STRENGTH
- INCREASED AGILITY
- ENHANCED ENDURANCE
- ABILITY TO STICK TO SURFACES/WALLS
- SPECIAL "SPIDER-SENSE" WARNS OF DANGER

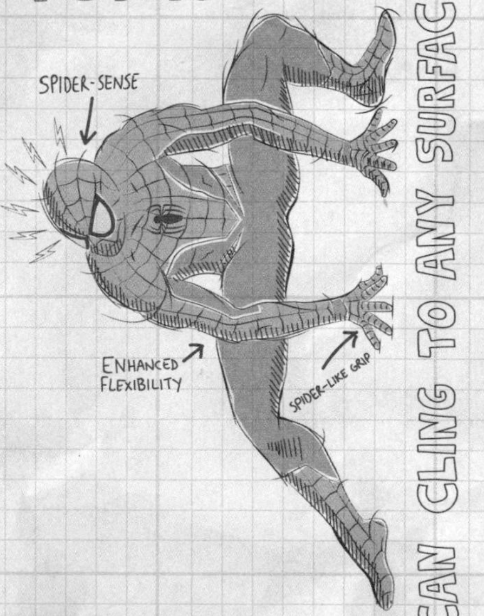
SPIDER-SENSE
ENHANCED FLEXIBILITY
SPIDER-LIKE GRIP
CAN CLING TO ANY SURFACE

I decided to document this new experience. Setting up my camera in a deserted alley, I tested out my newfound "abilities."

Analysis?

I am **LITERALLY** climbing up the walls!

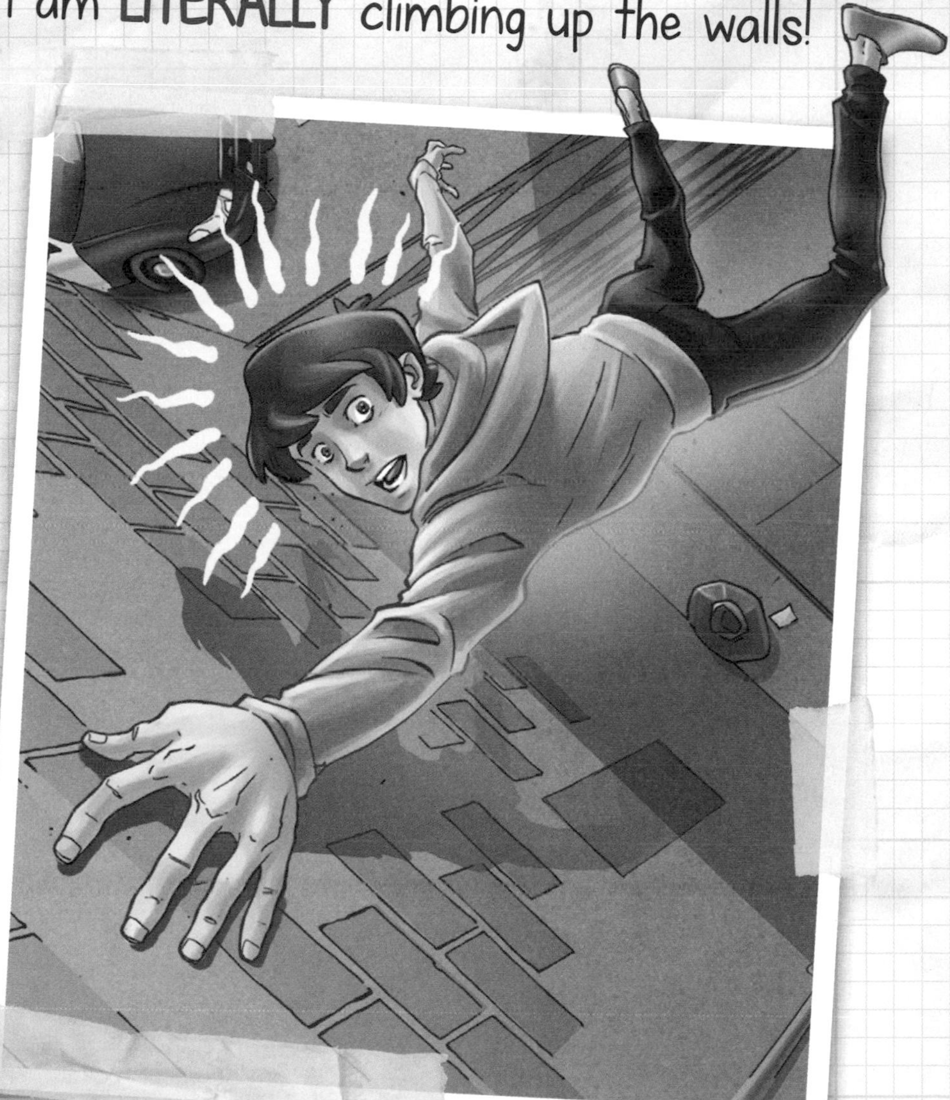

JOURNAL ENTRY 3:

Usually, when things get nuts, I go to Uncle Ben for advice. He really believes in me even when I don't believe in myself. When he said I was meant to do great things...I figured it would be winning best science experiment...not BEING the science experiment.

Another thing he always tells me is:

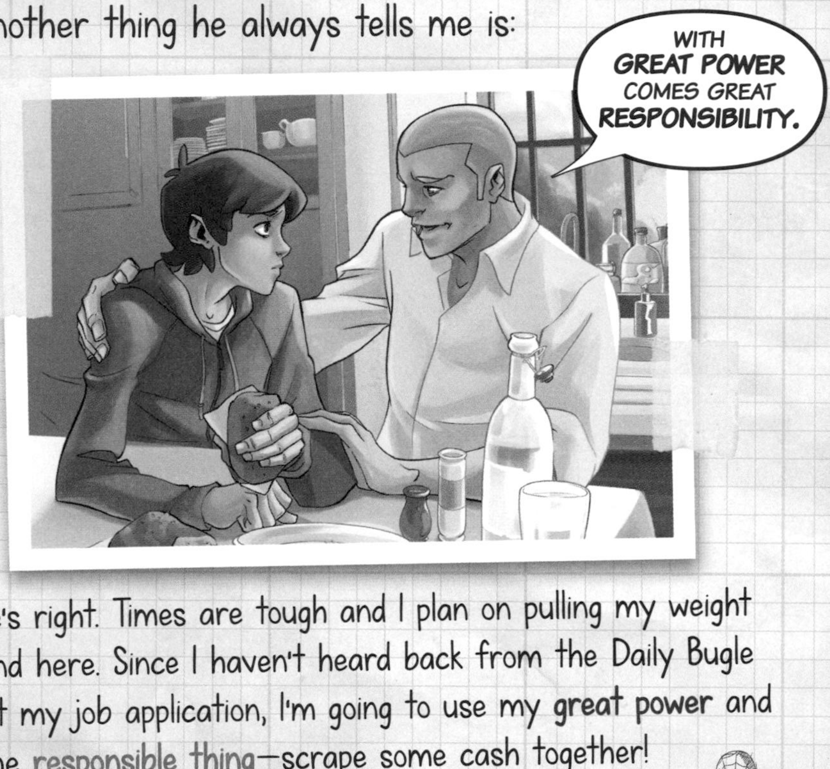
WITH **GREAT POWER** COMES GREAT **RESPONSIBILITY.**

He's right. Times are tough and I plan on pulling my weight around here. Since I haven't heard back from the Daily Bugle about my job application, I'm going to use my **great power** and do the **responsible thing**—scrape some cash together!

But first, I'll need a great costume to conceal my identity.

COSTUME DESIGN IDEAS

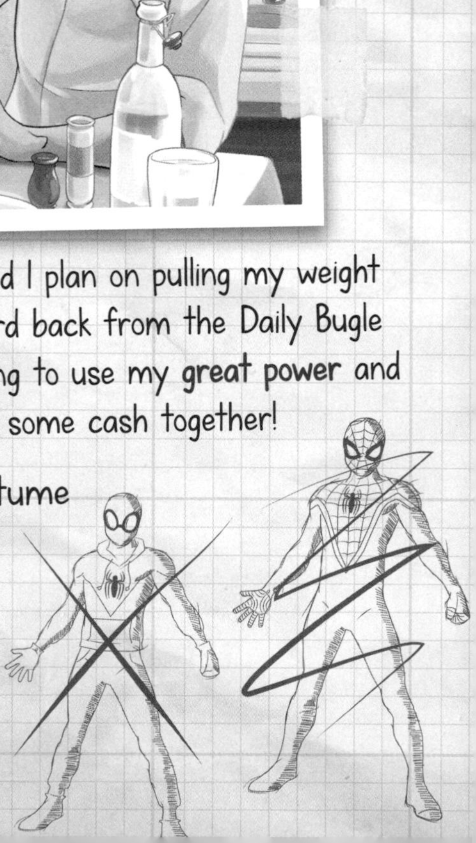

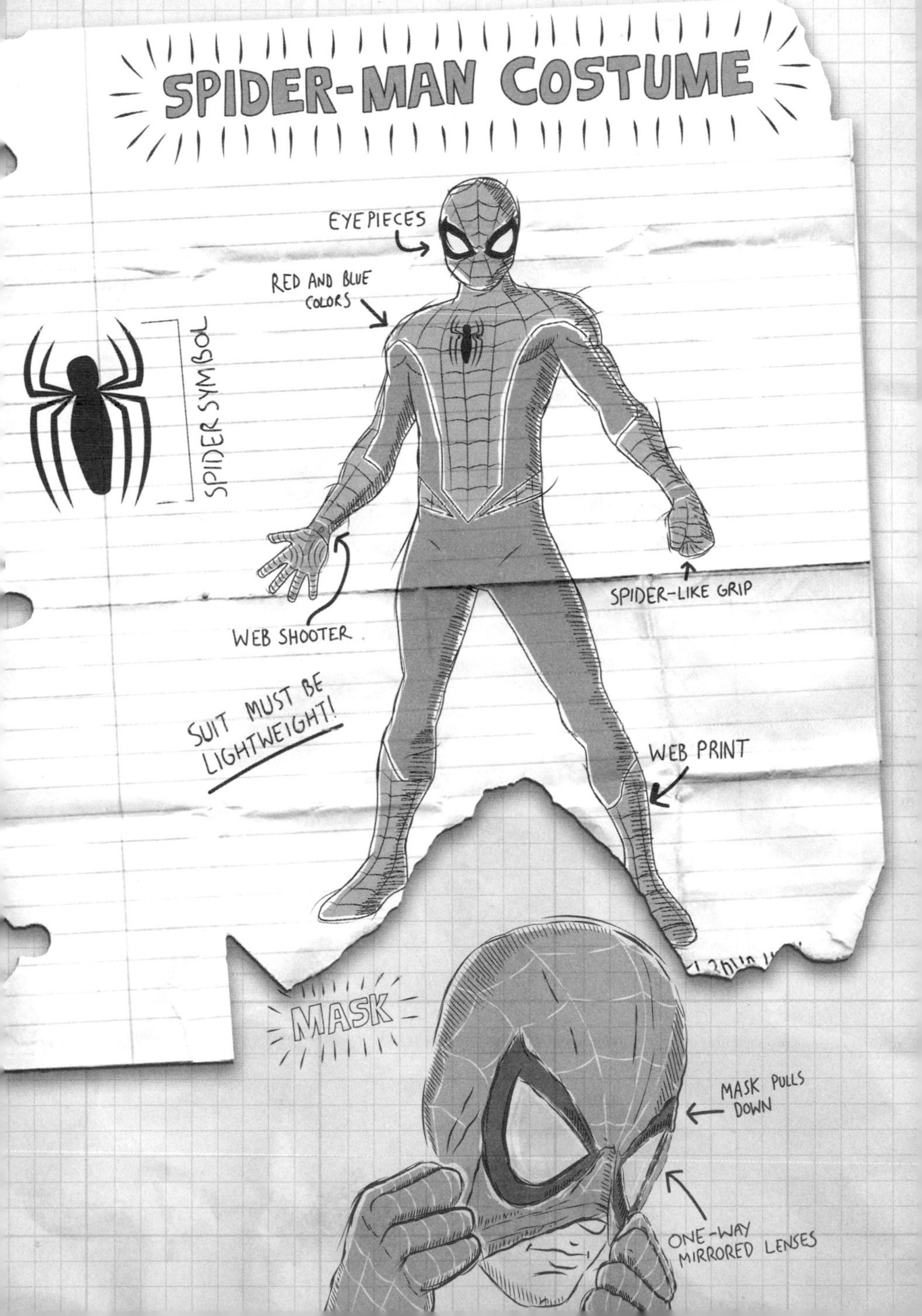
SPIDER-MAN COSTUME
EYEPIECES
RED AND BLUE COLORS
SPIDER SYMBOL
SPIDER-LIKE GRIP
WEB SHOOTER
SUIT MUST BE LIGHTWEIGHT!
WEB PRINT
MASK
MASK PULLS DOWN
ONE-WAY MIRRORED LENSES

JOURNAL ENTRY 4:

When I was a kid, Uncle Ben would take me to watch Global Wrestling, his favorite wrestling league, whenever they were in the city. Crusher Hogan was by far the best wrestler out there. He was nearly undefeated until...

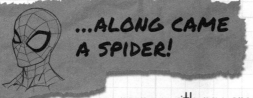

...ALONG CAME A SPIDER!

So today, I had an idea. I'm pretty sure the best way to make money with my amazing abilities without raising suspicion is as a professional wrestler. Global Wrestling is back in town looking for new talent, so I signed up for my first fight, which happened to be this evening. Crusher Hogan was headlining the event and I was trembling in my tights at the thought of meeting him. That's when I was inspired to give myself the ominous moniker **SPIDER-MAN** to strike fear into my foes. **Bwahahah!**

I was the gangliest guy there. And yet, with my speed, strength, and smarts, I made it up the ranks to face Crusher himself! He sized me up, laughing about how he was going to "CRUSH ME LIKE A BUG."

To be honest, I felt kind of bad picking Crusher up and swinging him around like a rag doll. Guess what?

The prize money helped me get over it!

SPIDER-MAN IS A KNOCK-OUT!

anuary
or abo low enough.

tted
ying
pace
cities
er the
ivers.

range
stors.

vagen
s with
tt, an
rator.

pple's
ailing
uxing.

500m
evelop
g cars.

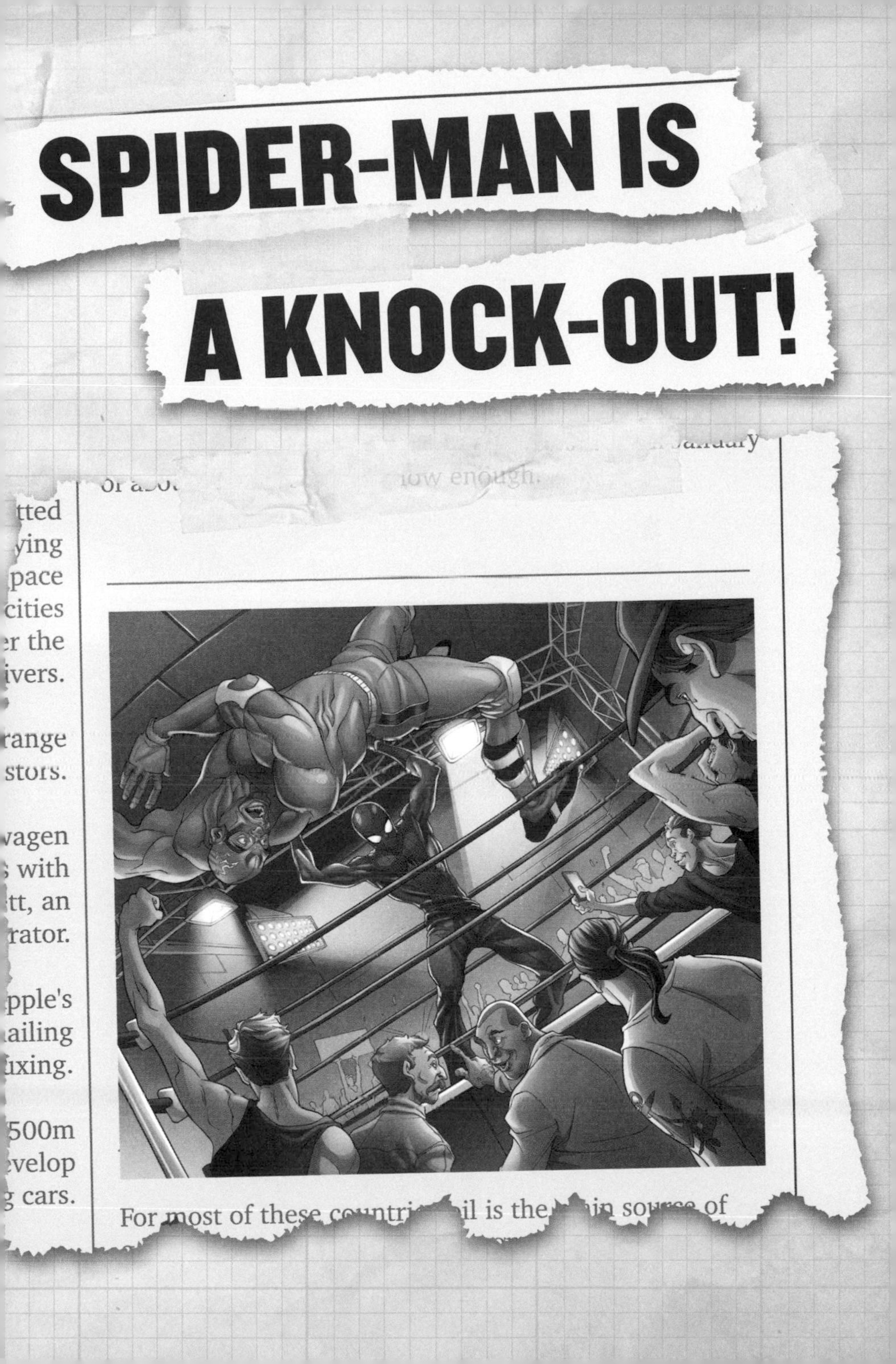

For most of these countri il is the in source of

JOURNAL ENTRY 5:

Thanks to my bout with Crusher Hogan, I am **CRUSHING** it! "Spider-Man" has spun a web of intrigue, but it's not enough. He needs a gimmick to make him even more sensational and spider-like. He needs to make webs for real.

So, with my newfound riches, I have purchased the following items:

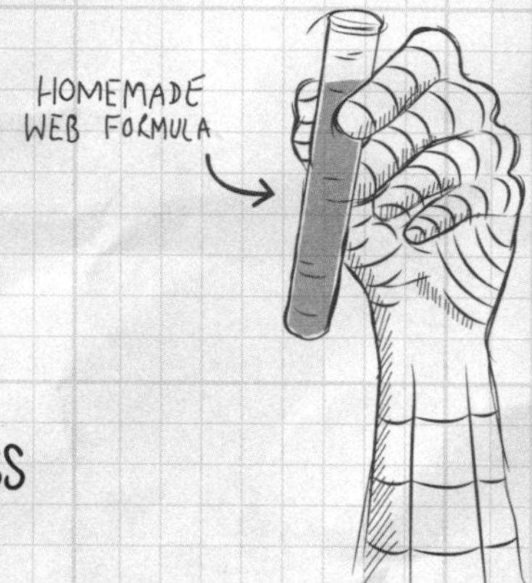
HOMEMADE
WEB FORMULA

- STAINLESS STEEL TUBES
- SMALL TURBINE PUMP VANES
- A BLOCK OF TEFLON
- NICKEL-PLATED ANNEALED BRASS
- SOLENOID-NEEDLE VALVE
- CHEMICAL COMPOUNDS FOR MY "WEBS"
- TRIGGER SWITCHES
- BAND OF SPRING STEEL

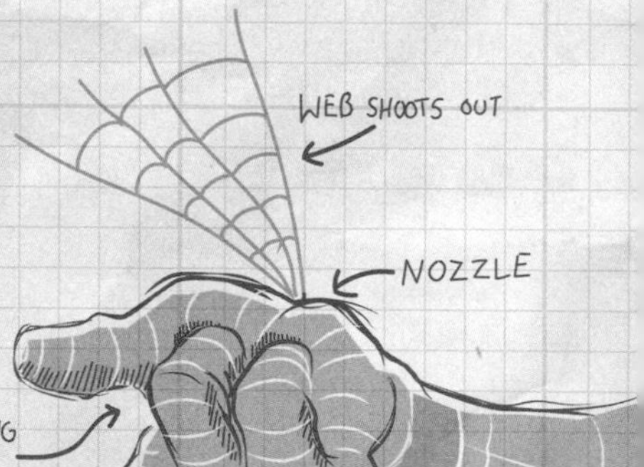
WEB SHOOTS OUT
NOZZLE
FIRE BY PRESSING
FINGERS TO PALM

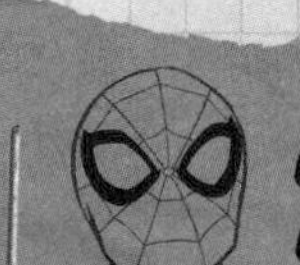

WELL, ONLY A SCIENCE WHIZ COULD HAVE CREATED A DEVICE LIKE THIS!

After countless equations and experiments, my "web-shooters" are complete and ready for action. These twin devices are worn like wrist gauntlets under my costume and release thin strands of a special pressurized "web fluid"—nylon-like, tensile, and sticky—at incredible speeds!

WORST. DAY. EVER.

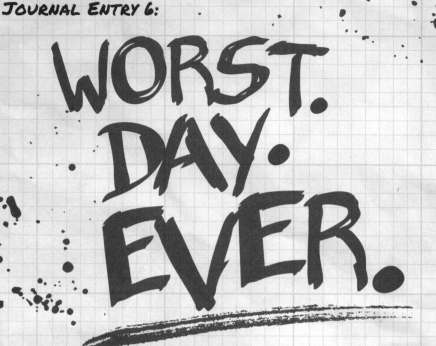

How could this happen? How is Uncle Ben DEAD!?

This morning Spider-Man was on top of the world, basking in his newfound celebrity. Tonight, Peter Parker's world came crashing down.

Earlier, as I was leaving the arena after my latest victory, I noticed the ticket office was being robbed. The burglar ran off while the manager screamed for me to stop him. I just shrugged and said, "Not my problem, dude." What a **JERK** I was.

When I got home, the house was surrounded by police cars. Aunt May was crying. I didn't need Spider-Sense to know something very bad had happened.

Then I learned the truth. The news hit me harder than any uppercut in the ring; Uncle Ben had confronted an armed robber. There was a struggle and a gunshot. The intruder escaped. Uncle Ben was dead.

(Even as I write this, I can't believe it's real.)

When a police scanner reported the suspect was cornered, I decided to take matters into my own hands.

SPIDER-MAN WOULD AVENGE BEN PARKER.

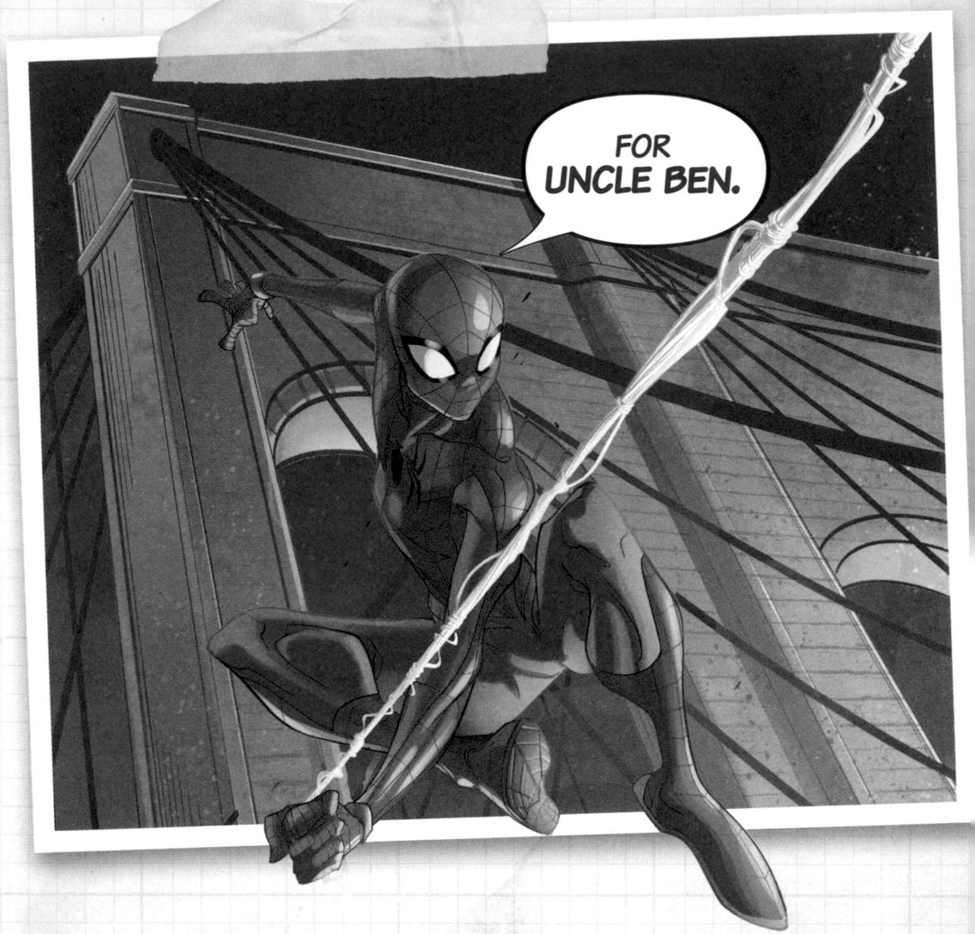
FOR
UNCLE BEN.

Swinging toward the coordinates, I found the killer holed up in an old warehouse. I planned on breaking every bone in his body... until I saw his face. My blood ran cold and my knees gave out.

It was the same guy that robbed the arena.
The same guy I could have stopped but didn't.

It's all **MY** fault. Uncle Ben is dead because of **ME.**

From now on, I vow to use my powers to protect others for as long as I have fighting breath left.

WEB OF INTRIGUE

MASKED MYSTERY MAN CATCHES CROOK UNCONVENTIONALLY!

low enough.

tted
ying
pace
cities
er the
ivers.

range
stors.

wagen
s with
tt, an
rator.

pple's
ailing
uxing.

500m
evelop
g cars.

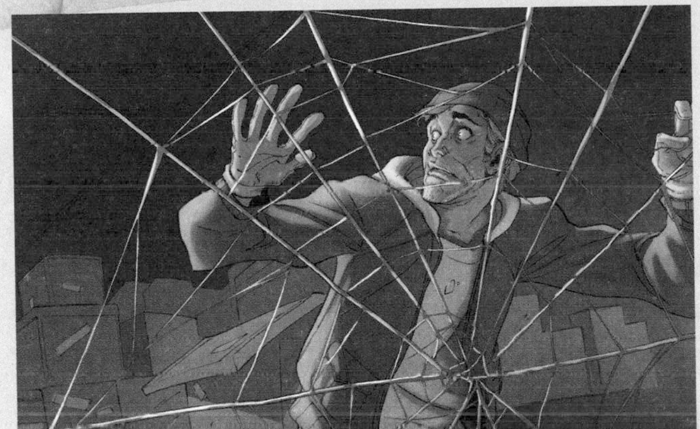
POLICE RENDERING

For most of these countri il is the in source of

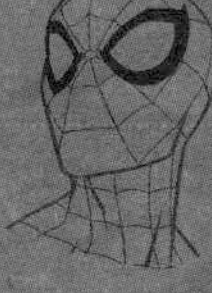

THANK GOODNESS THEY CAUGHT MY GOOD SIDE IN THAT SKETCH!

PETER PARKER'S **PORTFOLIO**

TO:
J. JONAH JAMESON
EDITOR-IN-CHIEF
@THE DAILY BUGLE

RE:
PHOTOGRAPHER
FOR HIRE

GUESS WHO JUST GOT HIRED BY THE BUGLE!!!!

← THIS GUY!

DAILY BUGLE

Peter Parker
Photographer

J. Jonah Jameson
Editor in Chief

PRESS

ID: 018125150

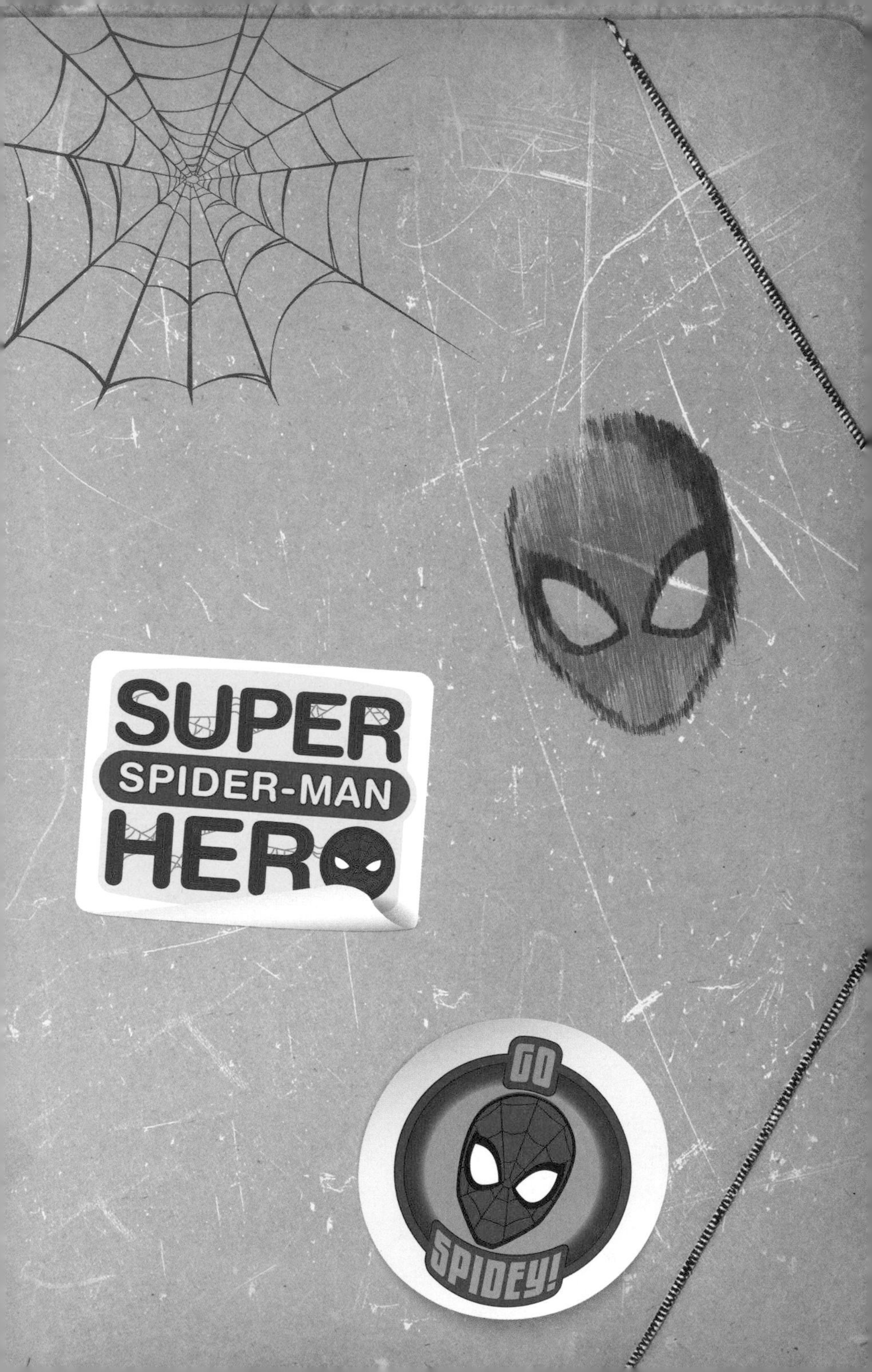
SUPER
SPIDER-MAN
HERO
GO
SPIDEY!

I can't believe it's only been a month since I became Spider-Man. In that short amount of time, my entire life has turned **upside-down** and yet, for Peter Parker, nothing has changed at all. I still have to study for my Chemistry exams, make it to class on time, and try really hard not to web Flash's mouth shut when he taunts me. It's so ironic that he has such a man-crush on Spider-Man and yet enjoys bullying me. I'll let him have his fun. Most of these dumb jocks peak in high school anyway...

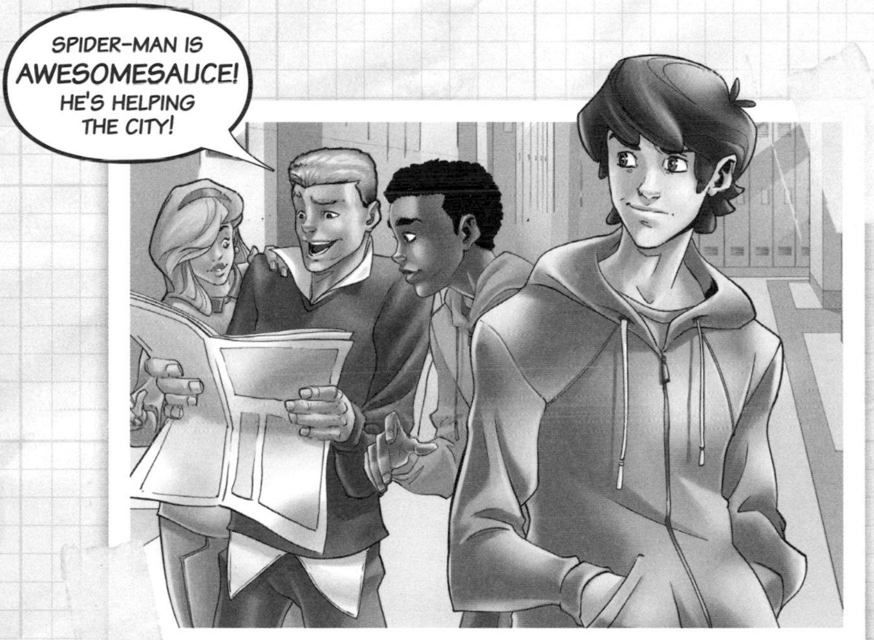
SPIDER-MAN IS AWESOMESAUCE! HE'S HELPING THE CITY!

But Flash has got me thinking. He may have a point about Spider-Man helping the city. Bringing Uncle Ben's murderer to justice was a selfish act of revenge for Peter Parker. Spider-Man, on the other hand, has become a symbol of heroism and hope. Maybe I can help change the city, pay it forward...**and pick up some extra cash along the way!**

JOURNAL ENTRY 7:

The city has been literally buzzing with rumors of other "super-powered" beings popping up.

Take this guy Max Dillon. The papers say he used to be just a regular guy working for the electric company until he was struck by lightning. Now, as a man made of living electricity, he calls himself **ELECTRO.** Problem is, he creates blackouts so he can go on crime sprees. Today, Electro and I crossed paths while I was swinging home from school as Spider-Man.

Electro had just blasted an armored truck and was looting the loot!

Swooping down, I made sure the driver was okay. Then I set up my camera to get prime pics of the action. Electro didn't like it when I lobbed a ball of web right at his head. He also didn't like it when I called him **"SPARKY"** and tried to tie him up in my web.

The high-voltage villain sizzled through it like it was paper. I webbed his hands even tighter, pulling him over to the fuse box on a nearby telephone pole. The surging electricity overloaded his nervous system and shut it down, knocking him out. This was a good thing, because I was all out of ideas... and needed to go home and study!

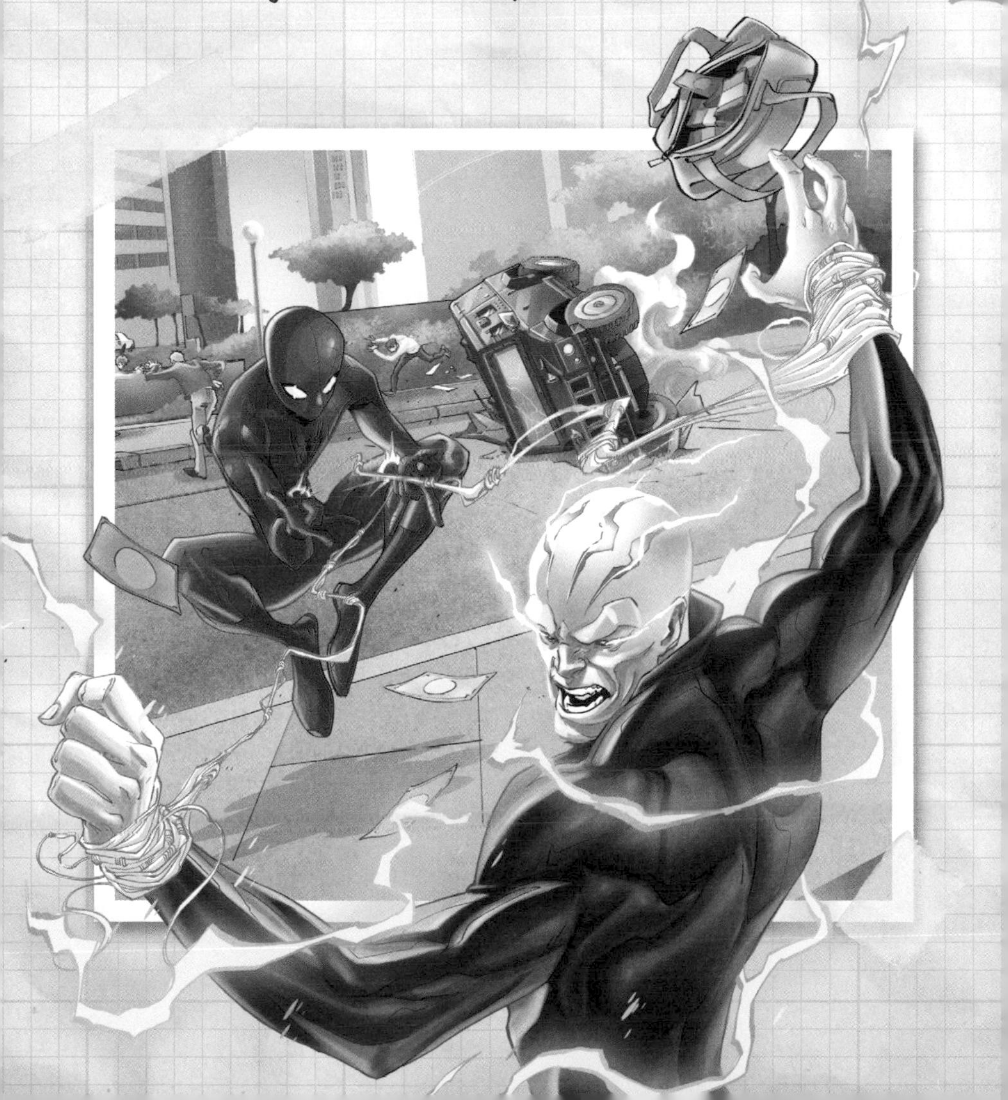

JOURNAL ENTRY 8:

Yesterday's battle with Sparky certainly brightened my mood! Not even my pompous **GAS-BAG** of a boss, J. Jonah Jameson, editor-in-chief of the Daily Bugle, could bring me down. So as I braced myself for one of his terrible tantrums, I was **shocked** (like the pun?) to see that he loved the photos I took of Spider-Man versus Electro. He loved them so much that he wanted me to go to the Policeman's Ball this evening and photograph the event for the paper.

I asked him what the catch was. His response?

"YOU'RE DOING IT FOR FREE."

I told him I was bringing Aunt May as my date or he could find another photographer. Begrudgingly, he agreed.

So the ball was pretty fancy. A lot of the city's officials and politicians were there. Jameson kept reminding me to be seen and not heard as well as not to embarrass him.

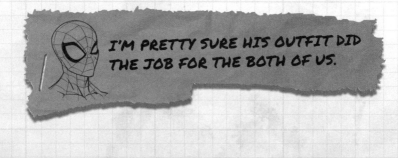

I'M PRETTY SURE HIS OUTFIT DID THE JOB FOR THE BOTH OF US.

After my third or fourth bacon-wrapped scallop, my Spider-Sense tingled. The ground began to shake violently and soon the source of the vibrations came into view. **ANOTHER CROOK IN A COSTUME!** This dude called himself the **SHOCKER!** As a bunch of off-duty cops charged at him, he raised his arms and blasted them away with waves of vibrating energy.

I rushed Aunt May out the door to safety. I could hear Jameson barking at me to take pictures. Don't worry, J.J. I set up my camera so I could come back and pose for my close-up as Spider-Man!

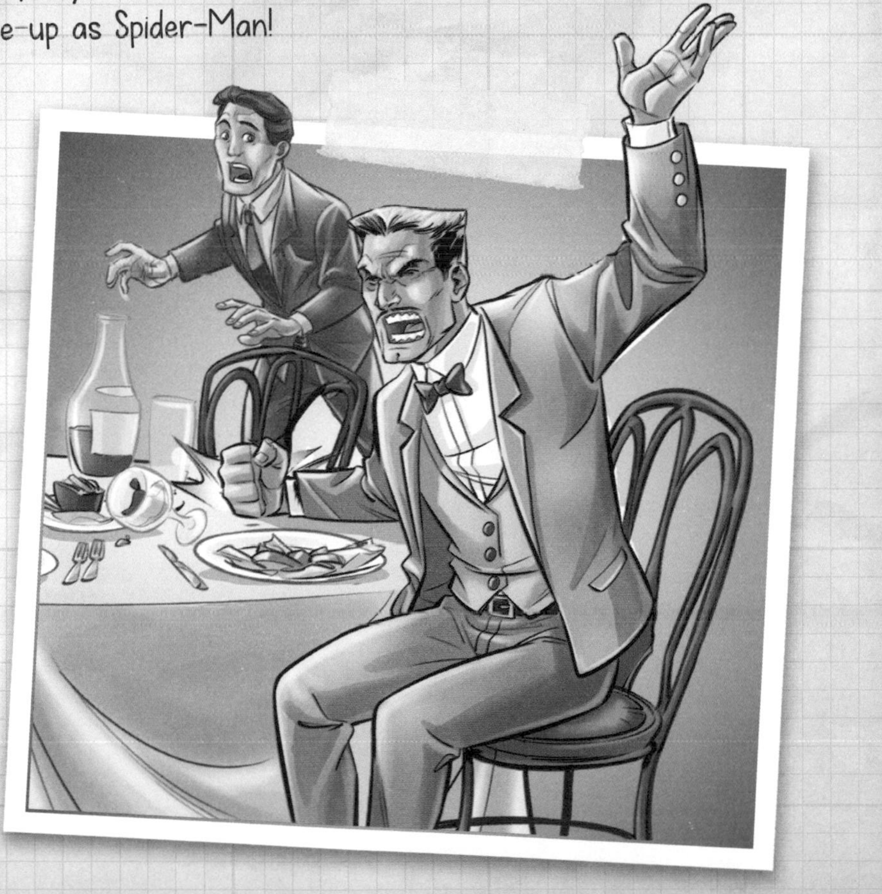

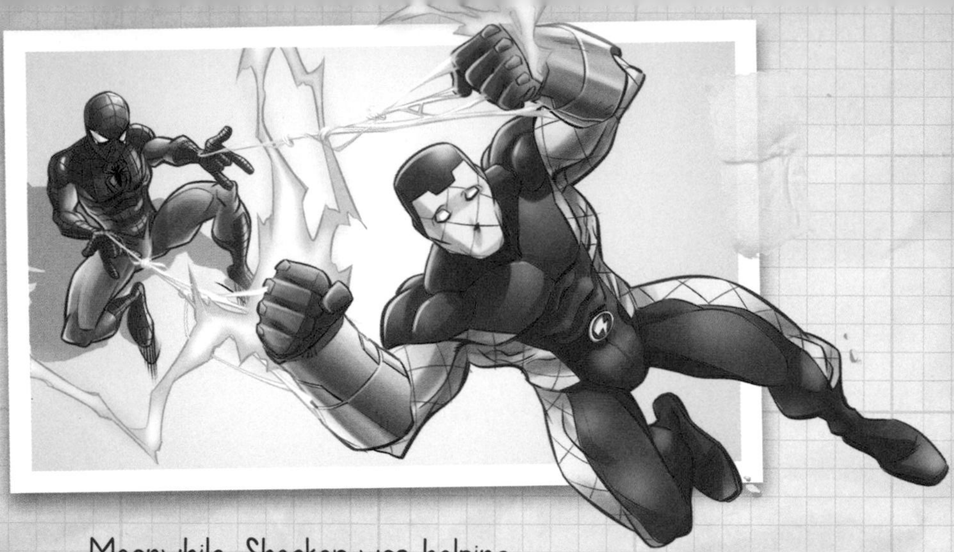

Meanwhile, Shocker was helping himself to the gold watches worn by the unconscious officers. Time for Spidey to crash the party, too. Shocker kept me at bay with his energy blasts. That gave me time to notice the shockwaves were being emitted from the gauntlets he was wearing.

I lassoed the gadgets with a webline and tore them off. Then I crunched them like soda cans. Bummer to destroy such neat high-tech artillery, but it put Shocker out of commission so the police could subdue him.

So, my experiences with Electro and Shocker made me realize there is a terrible trend of emerging enemies. I'm going to need all the info I can get on them, since knowing is half the battle!

I'm going to make a villain dossier!

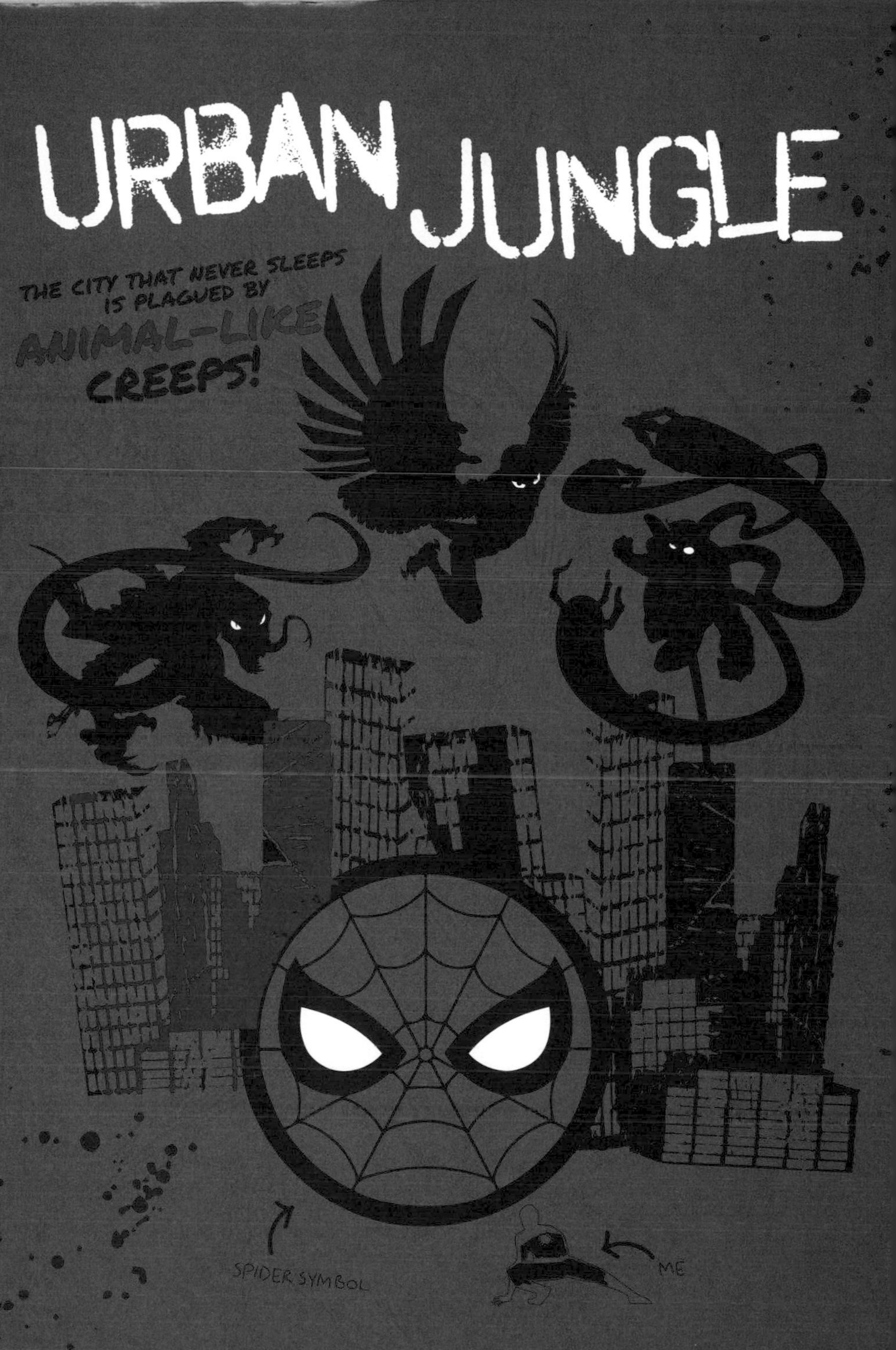
URBAN JUNGLE
THE CITY THAT NEVER SLEEPS IS PLAGUED BY ANIMAL-LIKE CREEPS!
SPIDER SYMBOL
ME

DOCTOR OCTOPUS

REAL NAME: OTTO OCTAVIUS

HEIGHT: 5'9" **WEIGHT:** 205 LBS.

POWERS & ABILITIES

- GENIUS-LEVEL INTELLECT IN ENGINEERING AND RADIATION
- HARNESS PROVIDES HIM WITH SUPERHUMAN SPEED AND AGILITY
- MECHANICAL ARMS CAN EXTEND THEIR LENGTH AND ARE EXTREMELY DURABLE
- ARMS ARE CAPABLE OF LIFTING SEVERAL TONS

Doctor Octavius was once a highly respected physicist and inventor. He created a harness with four mechanical tentacle-like arms that could be mentally controlled. Unfortunately, a lab accident fused the robotic appendages to his body and amplified Otto's arrogance to megalomaniacal levels. He now seeks to prove himself as the greatest criminal mind in the world under the nickname **DOCTOR OCTOPUS!**

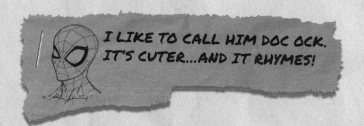

I LIKE TO CALL HIM DOC OCK. IT'S CUTER...AND IT RHYMES!

REAL OCTOPUS FACTS

- Octopuses are invertebrates, meaning they have no skeleton.
- Octopuses have two eyes, three hearts, and one beak.
- They are in a class of animals called "cephalopods," which means "head-feet" in Greek.
- Their main defense is camouflage as well as the excretion of a thick black ink cloud that conceals their escape from predators.

RHINO

REAL NAME: ALEKSEI SYTSEVICH

HEIGHT: 6'5"   **WEIGHT:** 710 LBS.

POWERS & ABILITIES

- POSSESSES SUPERHUMAN STRENGTH AND STAMINA
- SUIT OF ARMOR IS MADE OF A THICK, NEARLY INDESTRUCTIBLE POLYMER
- HORNS OUTFITTED TO ARMOR ARE CAPABLE OF PUNCTURING SOLID STEEL

Like Doc Ock, Aleksei became the subject of an ill-conceived illegal Mafia-run experiment gone awry...that bonded his body to a rhinoceros-like suit of armor. (Who comes up with this stuff? Not that I should talk...) The grueling trial endowed him with incredible strength that he uses with great relish in his continued criminal career as the rampaging **RHINO!**

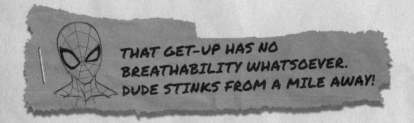

THAT GET-UP HAS NO BREATHABILITY WHATSOEVER. DUDE STINKS FROM A MILE AWAY!

REAL RHINO FACTS
- Rhinos can weigh almost 8,000 pounds.
- Relative to their large bodies, rhinos have small brains.
- Their horns are made from a protein called keratin— the same substance in fingernails!
- The word rhinoceros in Greek translates to "nose-horn."
- Rhinoceroses are herbivores, a.k.a. plant-eaters.

VULTURE

REAL NAME: ADRIAN TOOMES

HEIGHT: 5'11"   **WEIGHT:** 160 LBS.

POWERS & ABILITIES

- POSSESSES ADVANCED SKILLS IN ENGINEERING AND INVENTION
- WINGED HARNESS ALLOWS FOR FLIGHT AT HIGH SPEEDS AND SILENT MANEUVERABILITY
- METALLIC SUIT GRANTS SUPERHUMAN STRENGTH
- ALSO FEATURES RAZOR-SHARP TALONS CAPABLE OF TEARING THROUGH STEEL

Adrian Toomes is what would happen if the Wright Brothers had the WRONG idea! He was a gifted electrical engineer who wanted to make a man fly by successfully creating an electromagnetic pair of mechanical wings. Strapping them on, Toomes took to the skies—and terrorized New Yorkers by stealing anything his claws could carry as the vicious **VULTURE!**

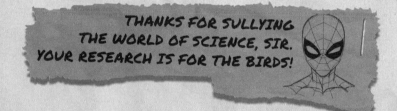

THANKS FOR SULLYING THE WORLD OF SCIENCE, SIR. YOUR RESEARCH IS FOR THE BIRDS!

REAL VULTURE FACTS

- Vultures can glide for hours on their wide, strong wings.
- They eat dead animals and are known as "nature's garbage-men."
- They can smell dead animals from a mile away.
- Their strong immune systems keep them from getting sick from spoiled meat!
- Vultures pee on their legs to keep cool (Ew!).

LIZARD

REAL NAME: CURTIS "CURT" CONNORS

HEIGHT: 6'8" **WEIGHT:** 550 LBS.

POWERS & ABILITIES

- SUPERHUMAN STRENGTH, AGILITY, AND DURABILITY

- THICK, SCALY HIDE PROVIDES RESISTANCE TO INJURY

- SAVAGE TEETH, SHARP CLAWS, AND WHIP-LIKE TAIL CAN INFLICT SERIOUS DAMAGE

- CAN MENTALLY COMMUNICATE WITH, AND CONTROL, NEARBY REPTILES

Not only was Dr. Connors a brilliant scientist and decorated wartime surgeon, he was one of my heroes. After he lost one of his arms in battle, he became obsessed with the regenerative ability of reptiles. Using lizard DNA, Dr. Connors developed a serum to regrow his arm—which it did—but with horrifying consequences. The formula transformed him into a reptilian creature driven by savage instinct. It is my mission to help Dr. Connors rid himself of his animalistic alter-ego... **THE LIZARD!**

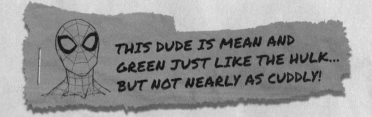

THIS DUDE IS MEAN AND GREEN JUST LIKE THE HULK... BUT NOT NEARLY AS CUDDLY!

REAL LIZARD FACTS

- Lizards are cold-blooded reptiles.
- Most lizards lay eggs.
- In many lizard species, if a tail is lost to a predator, it will grow back.
- Only two types of lizards are venomous; the Gila monster and the beaded lizard.
- The biggest lizard is the Komodo dragon. It can grow up to 10 feet long.

JOURNAL ENTRY 9:

I have been thinking a lot about how people deal with the bad things that happen to them. Especially brilliant, wealthy people that have the world at their fingertips. If Dr. Octavius and Dr. Connor can lose hope and turn to villainy...how is one of the little guys like me supposed to keep fighting the good fight?

We turn to our heroes. Tony Stark—owner of Stark Industries and armored Avenger **IRON MAN**—has been my idol for as long as I can remember. He's made breakthrough after breakthrough in the fields of science, engineering, and biomechanics. He's made Stark Towers here in NYC the new home of the Avengers, and it feels good knowing that a team of super heroes is watching over us.

Stark Industries was funding the annual Protection of Endangered Animals conference and I nearly jumped out of my skin when Jameson told me to cover this "fluff piece" for the paper.

King T'Challa, compassionate ruler of the African nation of Wakanda and scientific genius, was giving the keynote speech. If that isn't enough to make you sweat through your Spidey suit...he's also the super hero **BLACK PANTHER!**

T'Challa had just finished speaking when two snarling cheetahs roared and leaped into the crowd.

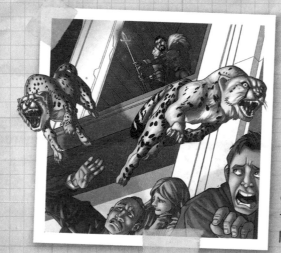

A costumed kook bellowed that he was **KRAVEN THE HUNTER** and he was out to catch the Black Panther! The Wakandan Warrior changed into his battle armor and charged at Kraven. Little did Lord Leopardprint know that a spider was about to ROCK this cat's cradle.

So there we were, Black Panther and Spider-Man, trying to herd cats. No big deal. I kept reminding myself not to geek out and to focus on the task at hand; keeping the cheetahs contained.

REAL PANTHER FACTS
- They are known as "the ghosts of the forest" because their dark coats helps them stalk prey at night.
- Panthers are the strongest tree climbers of the big cats.
- Black panthers in Asia and Africa are leopards. In the Americas, they are jaguars.
- Panthers are excellent swimmers.

King T'Challa, compassionate ruler of the African nation of Wakanda and scientific genius, was giving the keynote speech. If that isn't enough to make you sweat through your Spidey suit...he's also the super hero **BLACK PANTHER!**

T'Challa had just finished speaking when two snarling cheetahs roared and leaped into the crowd.

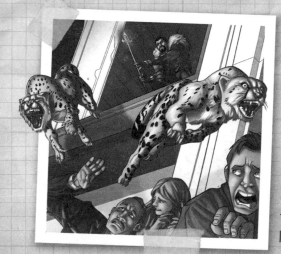

A costumed kook bellowed that he was **KRAVEN THE HUNTER** and he was out to catch the Black Panther! The Wakandan Warrior changed into his battle armor and charged at Kraven. Little did Lord Leopardprint know that a spider was about to ROCK this cat's cradle.

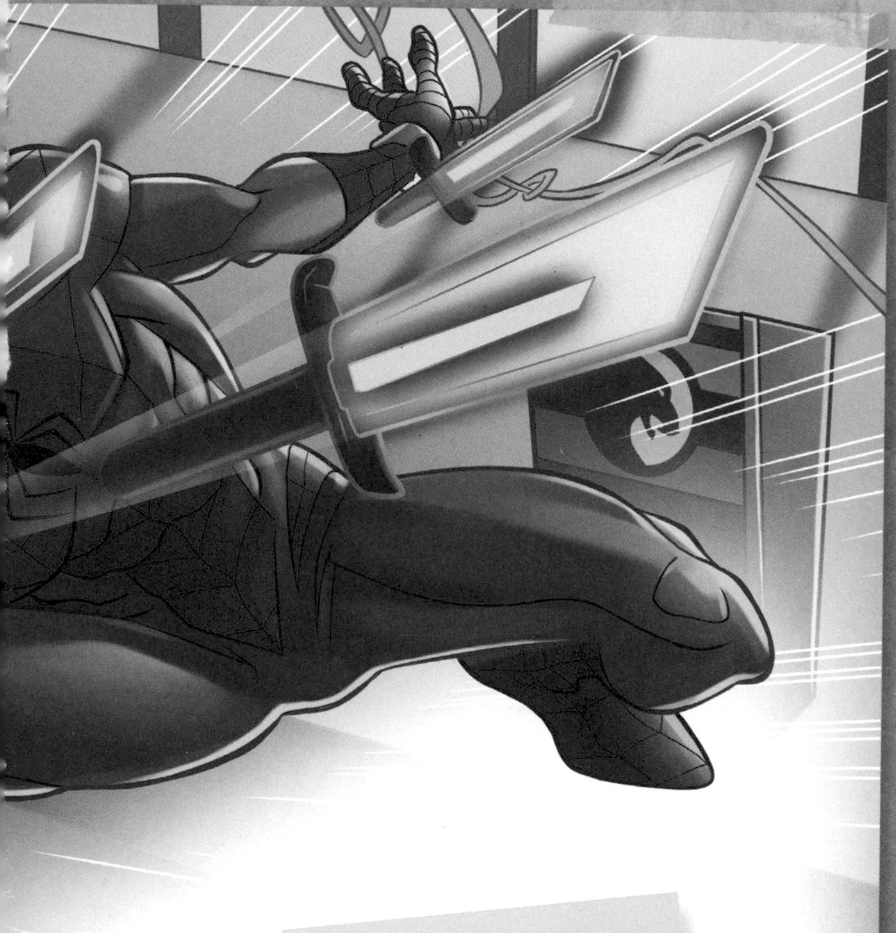

Kraven decided to sharpen his hunting skills on me.

Easy, huntsman...

I GET THE POINT!

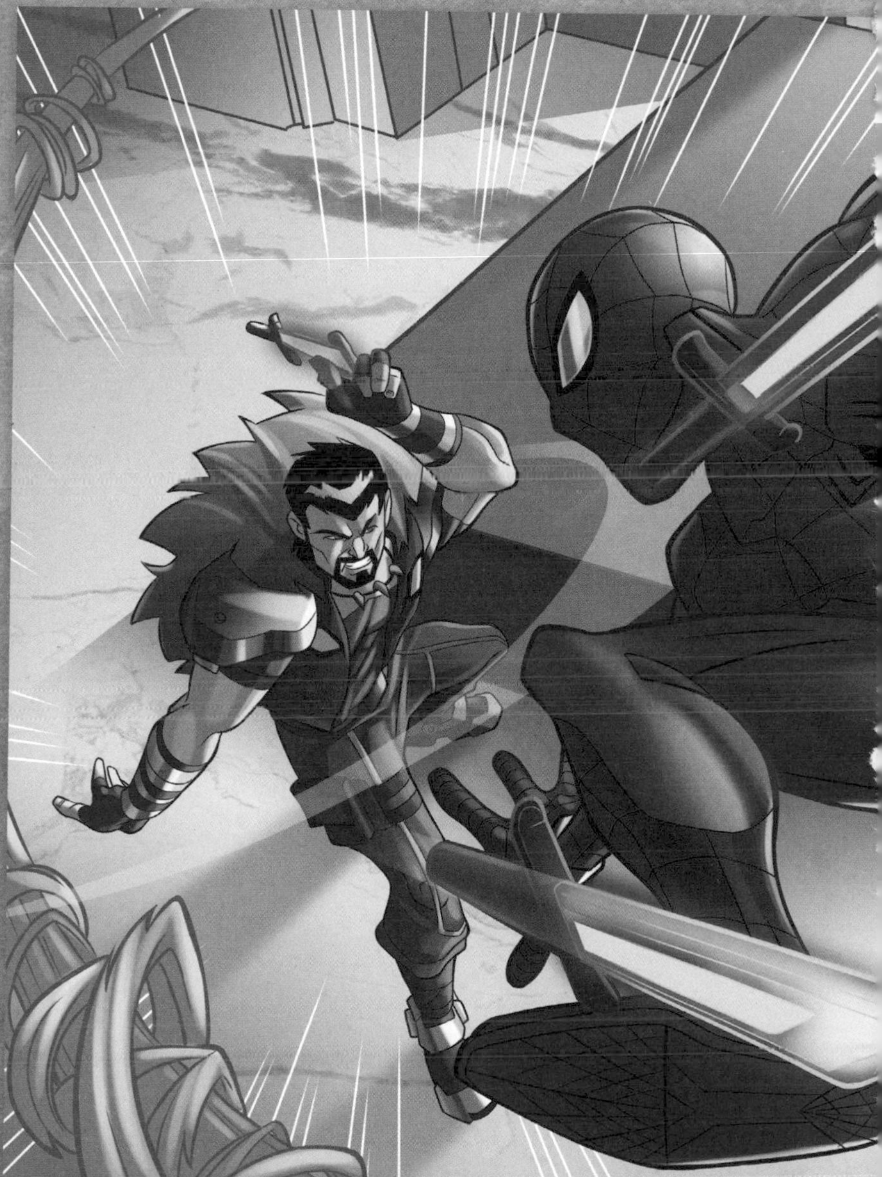

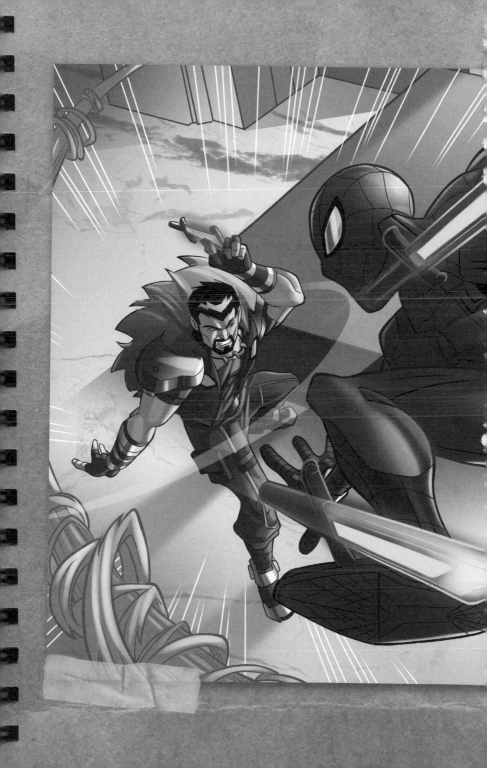

So there we were, Black Panther and Spider-Man, trying to herd cats. No big deal. I kept reminding myself not to geek out and to focus on the task at hand; keeping the cheetahs contained.

REAL PANTHER FACTS
- They are known as "the ghosts of the forest" because their dark coats helps them stalk prey at night.
- Panthers are the strongest tree climbers of the big cats.
- Black panthers in Asia and Africa are leopards. In the Americas, they are jaguars.
- Panthers are excellent swimmers.

Kraven was trussed up tight and ready for a cage of his own. The crowd cheered and Black Panther thanked me for my help. I was humbled by the king's kind words. I wanted to find the most dignified, appropriate words to tell his majesty that it was an honor just being in his presence, and that fighting alongside a living legend was a privilege. And yet, I was rendered speechless.

The only thing I managed to blurt out was...

SELFIE!

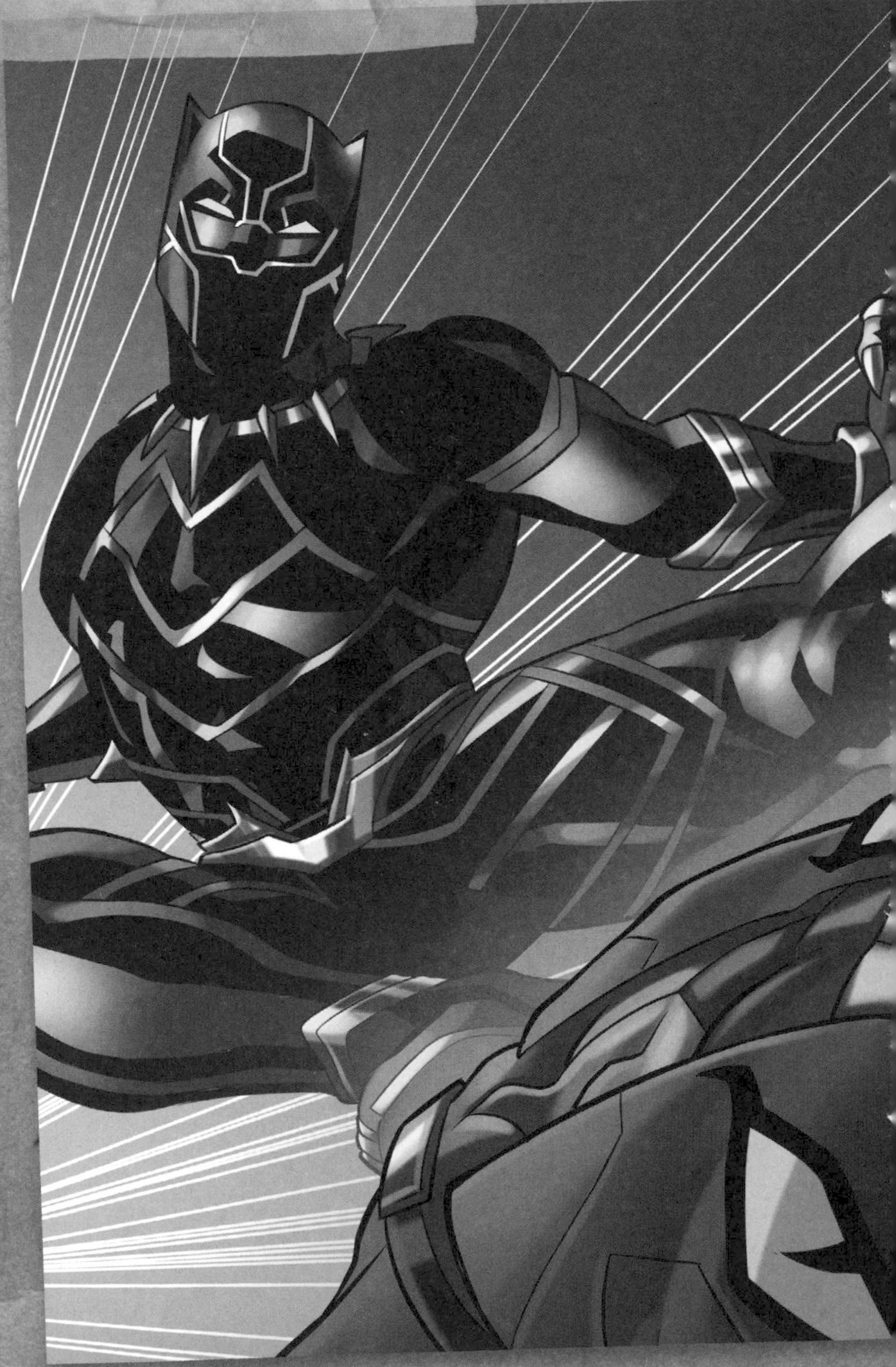

Good Samaritan that he is, Black Panther helped Kraven
KICK
his bad habit of being a bad guy!

Black Panther grabbed one of the cheetahs and held it tight before it could use me as a scratching post. His animal instincts told him the creatures were being used against their will. Kraven somehow increased their aggression, but Black Panther used his superior knowledge of wildlife to calm them down. It was an amazing thing to watch! The Wakandan Warrior safely pressed down on the cheetah's pressure points to relax their anger. Soon they were purring like kittens!

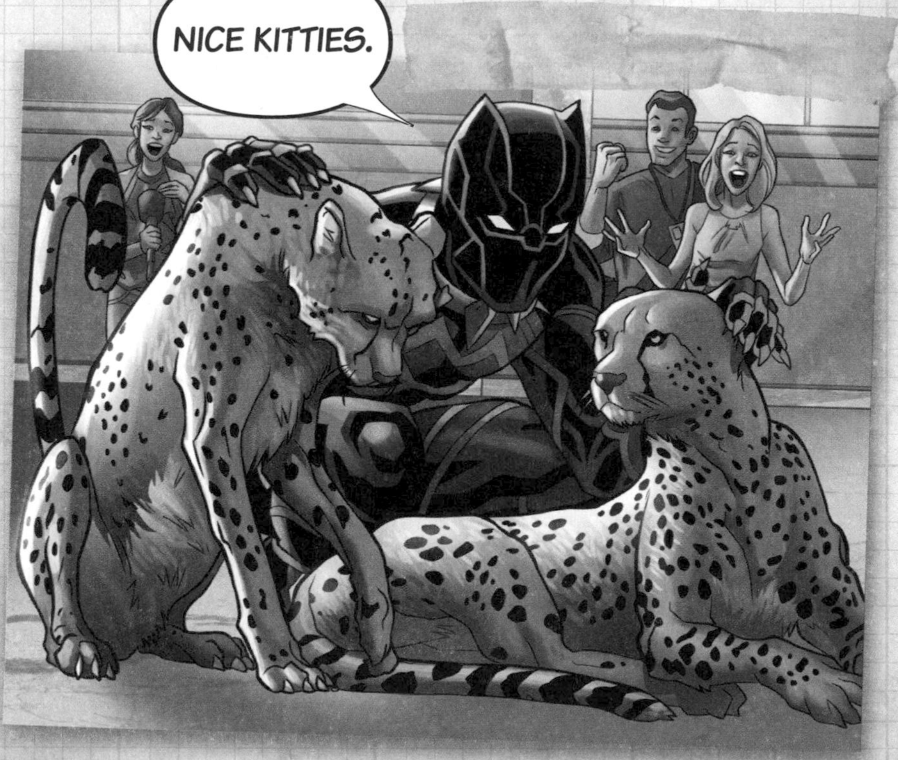
NICE KITTIES.

JOURNAL ENTRY 10:

I'm still geeking out over my meeting with the Black Panther. How does anyone calm down after all that excitement?

Today, I literally still had my head in the clouds. I was swinging over the city back home to Queens as Spider-Man. Suddenly, my Spider-Sense tingled and I swerved out of harm's way...just as a familiar feathered foe rocketed past me; the Vulture! Then, a red and gold bullet streaked by...**IRON MAN!**

Oh, boy, I smelled another team-up!!

With my camera at the ready I giddily gave chase, hoping to prove that I could play on the Super Hero varsity team, too.

With our combined forces, Iron Man and I clipped the Vulture's wings.

What a rush! Iron Man put his arm around me and thanked me. I nearly passed out, but I had to memorize every single moment of the exchange so I could transcribe it here verbatim:

IRON MAN: We make a pretty good team, kid. Some of the best victories are won when heroes work together. There's no shame in asking for help.

SPIDER-MAN: You're welcome, Mr. Stark.

IRON MAN: Mr. Stark was my father. Call me Tony!

(I could feel myself blushing under the mask. If I took it off, my face would still be the same color!)

Just then, as if on cue, the living legend himself—**CAPTAIN AMERICA**—somersaulted through the air and landed between me and Iron Man. I needed to sit down. This was just too much awesome.

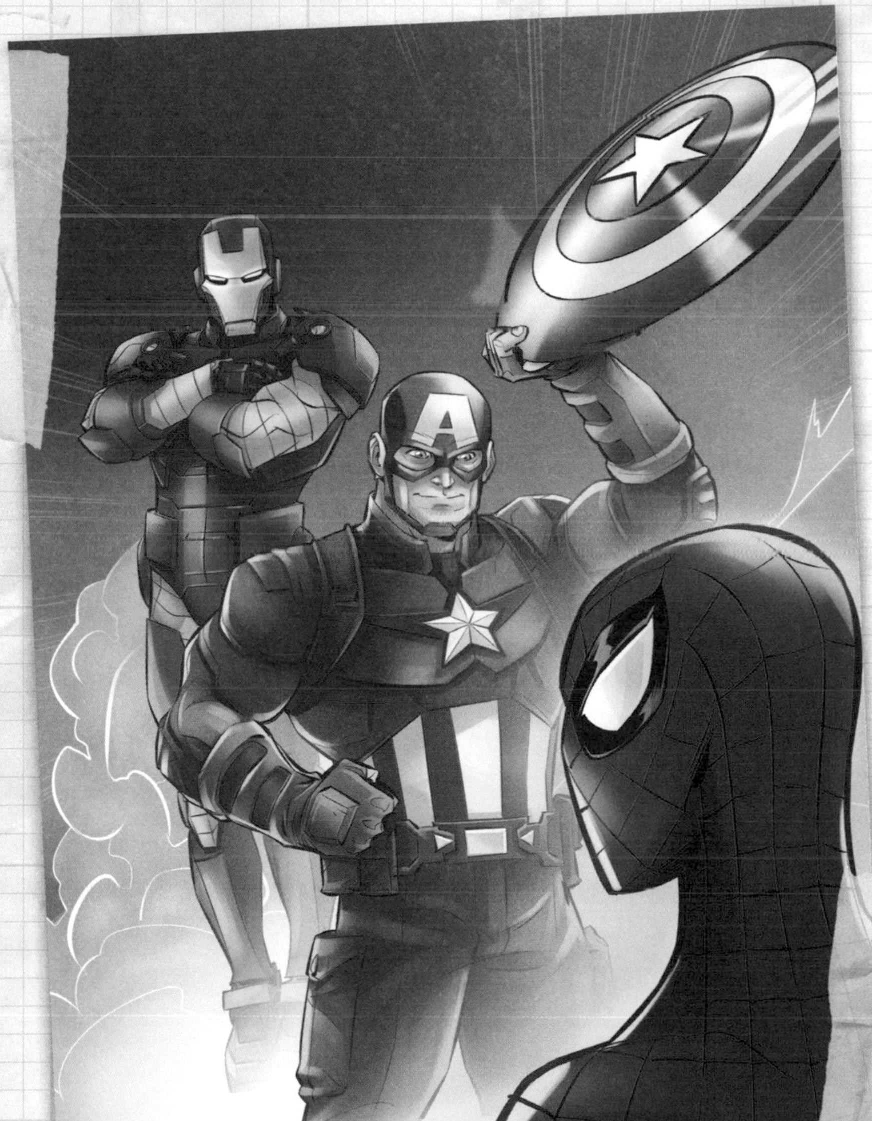

The super soldier had arrived to help Iron Man. Oops, guess I beat him to the punch. I was expecting a stern lecture for getting in the way of official Avengers' business. Instead, he was super chill. It was an excellent exchange that I'm transcribing for posterity so I can read it over and over and over again!

CAPTAIN AMERICA: Thanks for the assist, son.
   You've got potential.

SPIDER-MAN: Does that mean I can join the team?!

CAPTAIN AMERICA: Ha! You've got heart, I'll give you that.
   What part of New York are you from?

SPIDER-MAN: Queens.

CAPTAIN AMERICA: I'm from Brooklyn. Though it was
   very different seventy-five years ago.

TAKIN' CARE OF BUSINESS SUITS

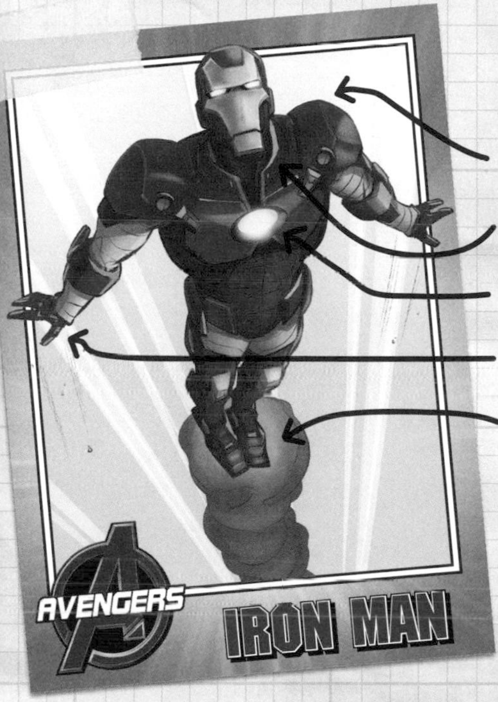
AVENGERS
IRON MAN

ARMORED ARSENAL

SMART MISSILES

HUD DISPLAY

VIBRANIUM CORE ARC REACTOR

REPULSOR RAYS

JET THRUSTERS

CAP'S KIT

VOICE-OPERATED WIRELESS COMMUNICATOR

RESISTANCE TO ELECTROSHOCK

ABSORBS FORCE OF IMPACT

ELECTROMAGNETIC VIBRANIUM SHIELD

UTILITY BELT

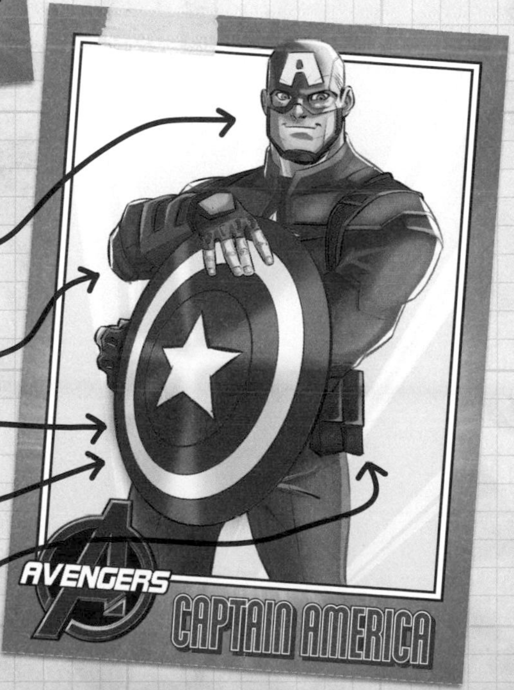
AVENGERS
CAPTAIN AMERICA

Wow, talk about the suit making the man! Cap and Iron Man have got it going on. I would love to make some upgrades to mine... But Stark is a billionaire and can create highly advanced suits of armor in his sleep. Maybe I can, too.

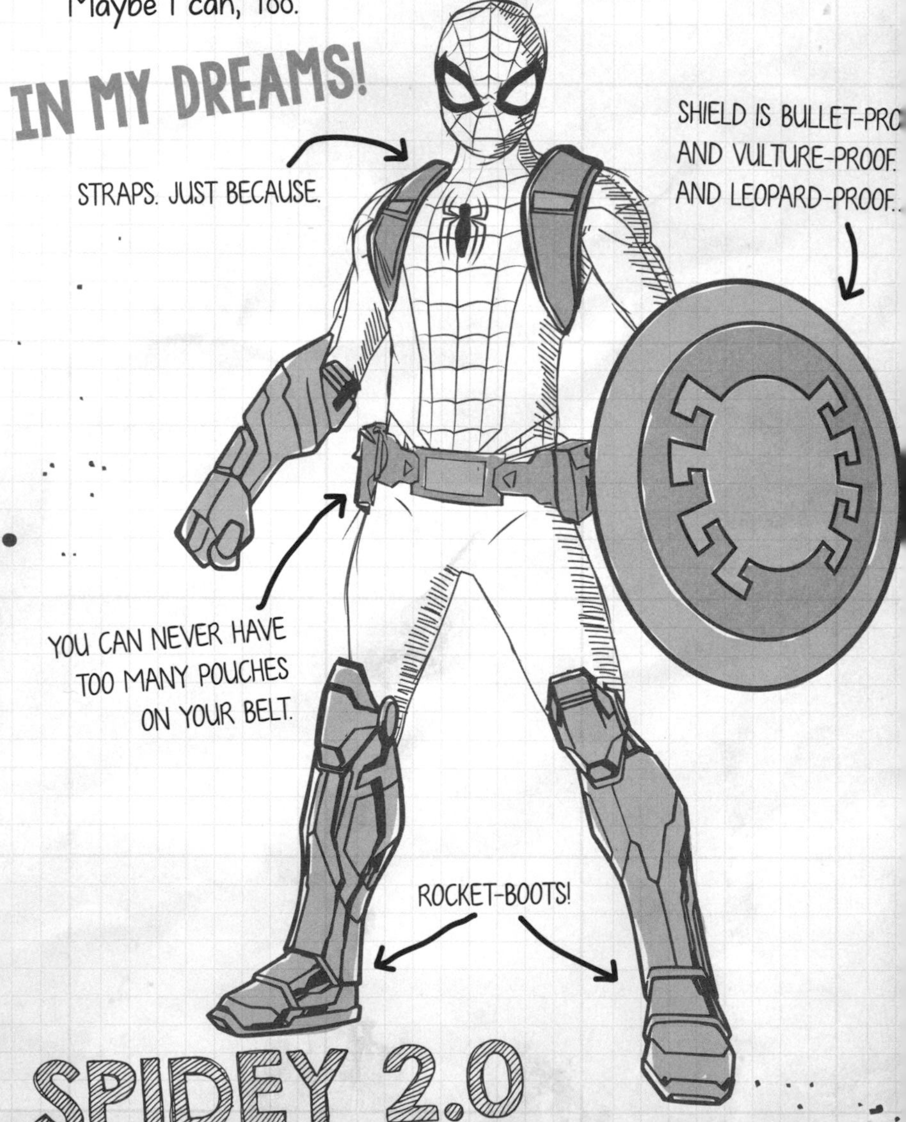

IN MY DREAMS!
STRAPS. JUST BECAUSE.
SHIELD IS BULLET-PRO
AND VULTURE-PROOF.
AND LEOPARD-PROOF...
YOU CAN NEVER HAVE
TOO MANY POUCHES
ON YOUR BELT.
ROCKET-BOOTS!
SPIDEY 2.0

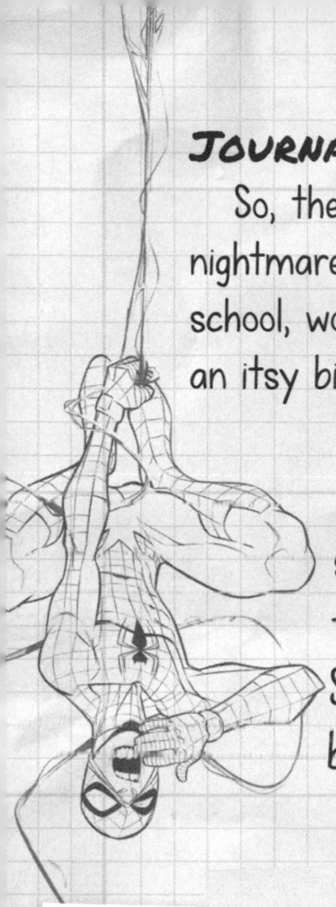

JOURNAL ENTRY 11:

So, the last couple of days have been a nightmare. I'm overwhelmed with balancing school, work, a nonexistent social life, AND an itsy bitsy thing called **BEING SPIDER-MAN!**

The anxiety had thrown me off my groove, so today I decided to see a specialist about the situation. Some think of him as the Sorcerer Supreme, but he prefers to be called **DOCTOR STRANGE.**

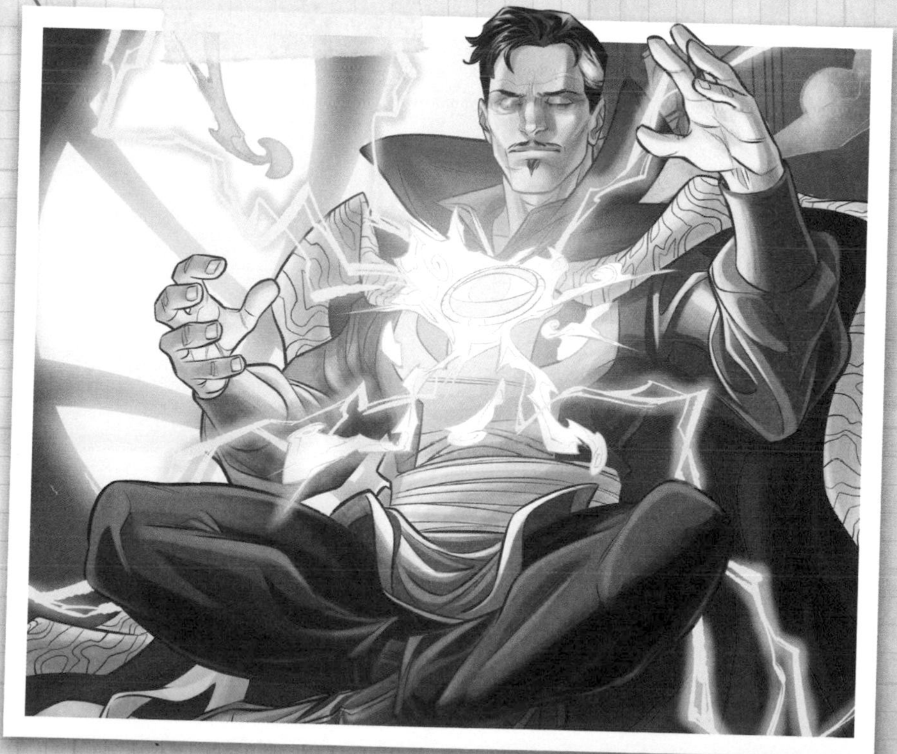

Before I even entered the doctor's Sanctum Sanctorum, he already knew why I was there. He's **that** good. Activating the **Eye of Agamotto**, an amulet whose light is used to negate evil magic, Doctor Strange put me to sleep and brought forth images of my dreams.

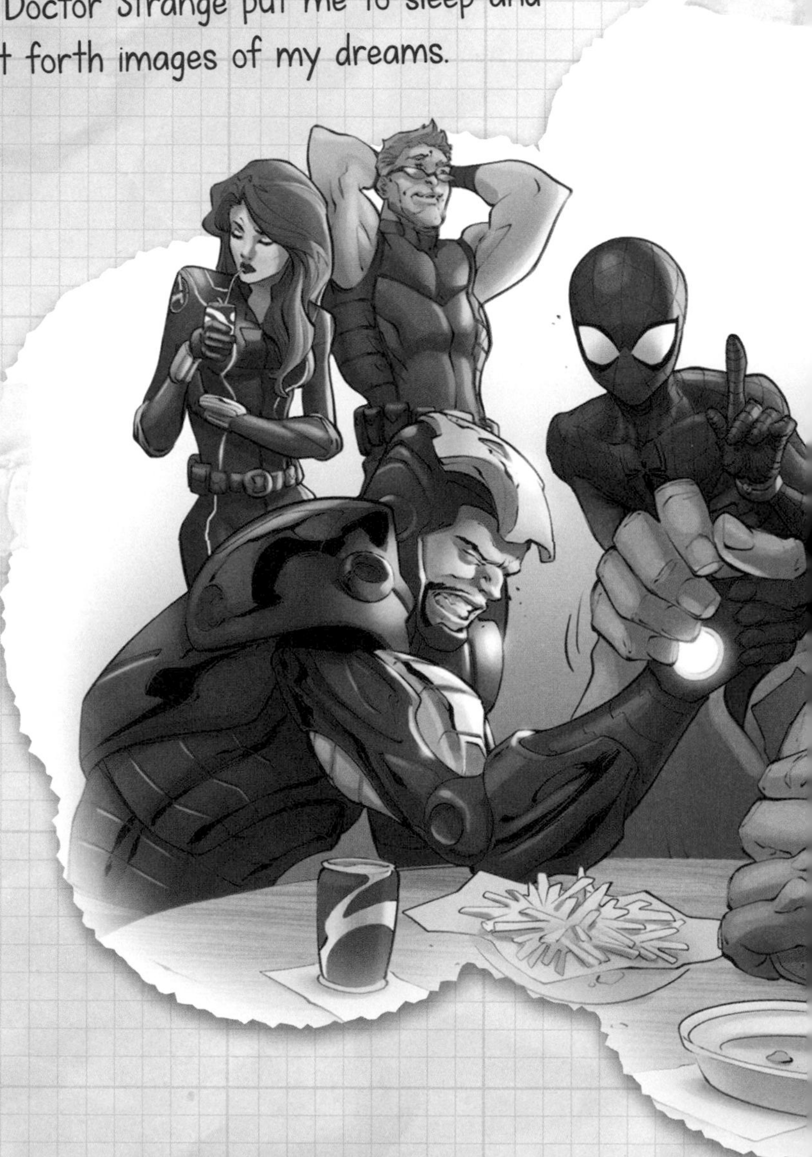

This first one was not that hard to analyze. It showed me hanging out with the Avengers, partaking in some of their awesome antics. That looked like a dream come true to me! The next scene, however, turned a bit sour...

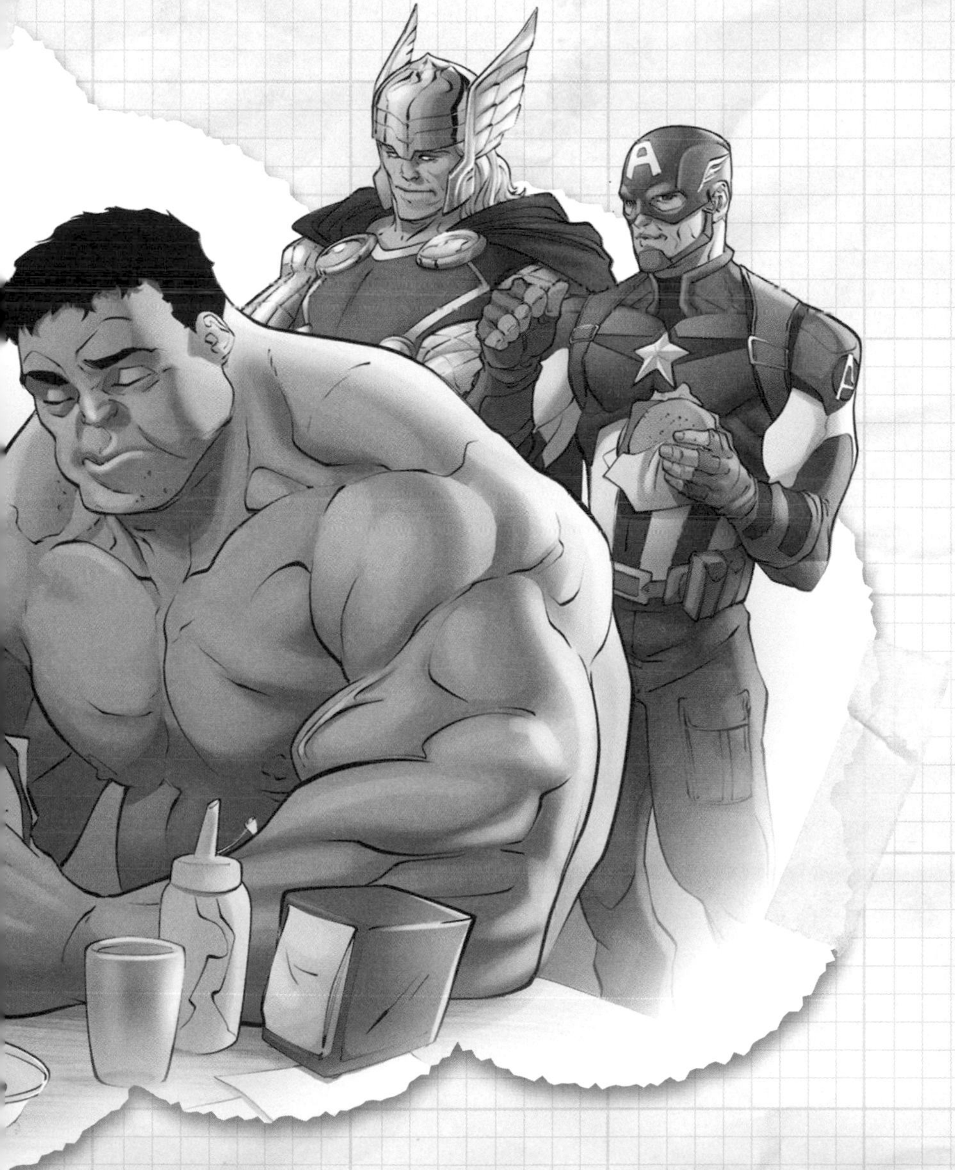

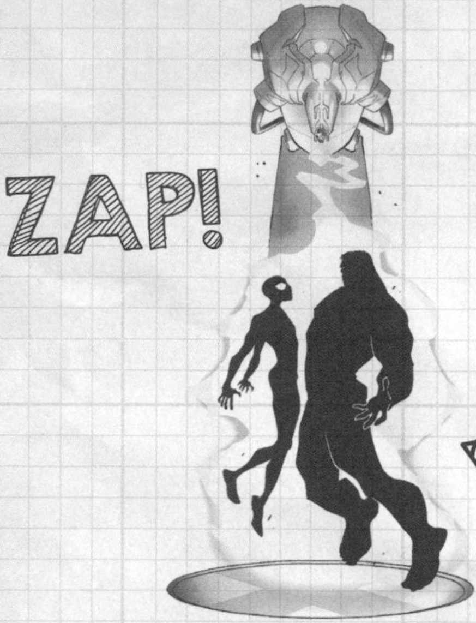
ZAP!

Spider-Man and Hulk were suddenly zapped by a radioactive energy beam that fused us together into some sort of **SPIDER-HULK!**

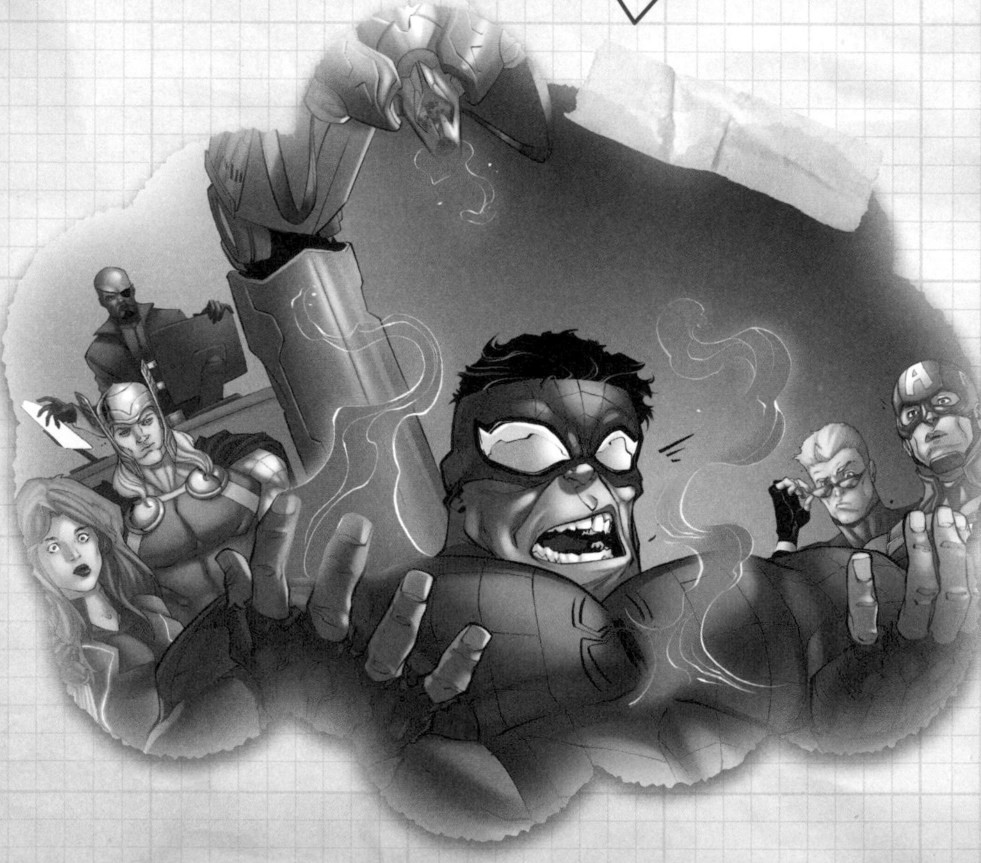

Spider-Hulk then went on a rampage through the city, eating everything in sight.

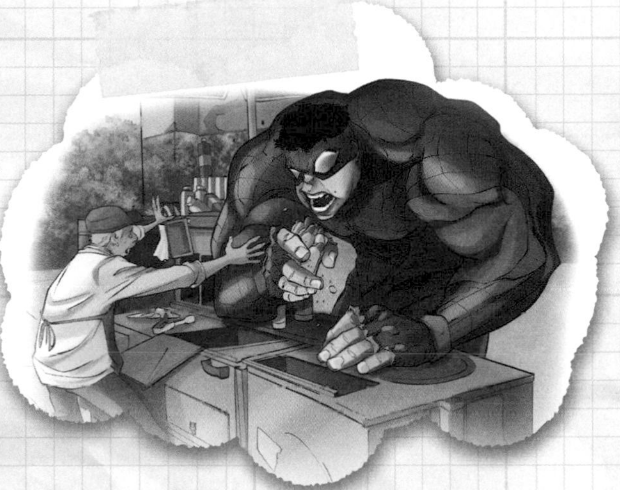

This caused the Avengers to give chase and try to stop us from doing any more damage!

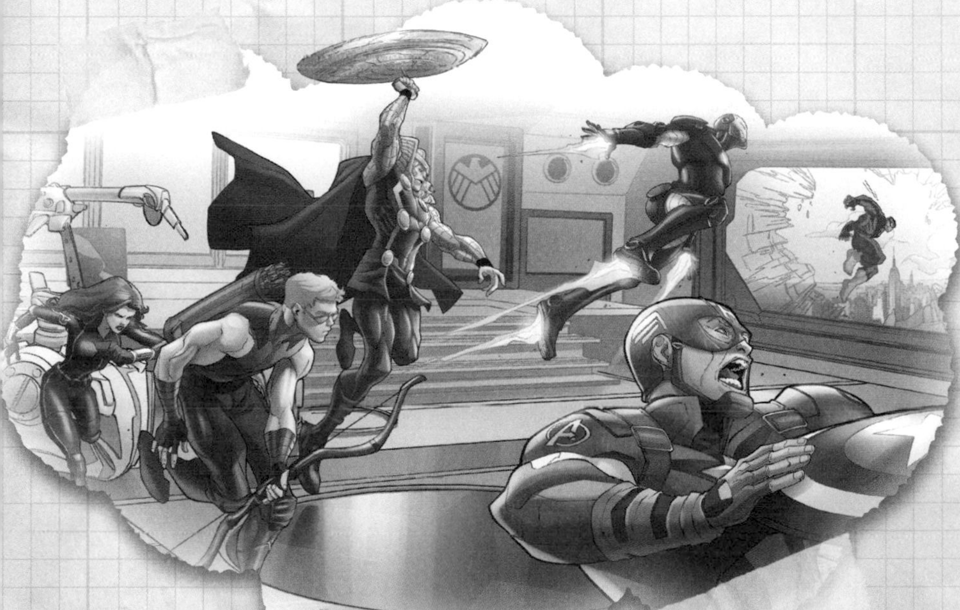

I could feel myself trying to swing on my webs, but I was too heavy and they snapped like threads. Spider-Hulk came hurtling down and **SMASHED** onto the street. That was when I jolted awake.

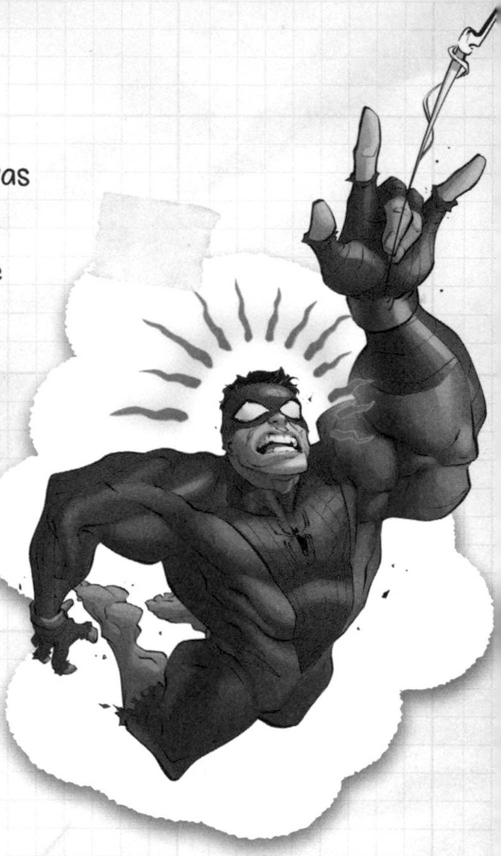

Doctor Strange's spell helped me realize that I had not really come to terms with my great power, nor the great responsibility that comes with it.

I've been green with envy that the Hulk is strong and powerful and unstoppable, but I am not the Hulk. I have to accept that even Spider-Man has his limitations. I should not beat myself up to be better. Peter Parker and Spider-Man have plenty of good combined and **THAT IS GOOD ENOUGH!**

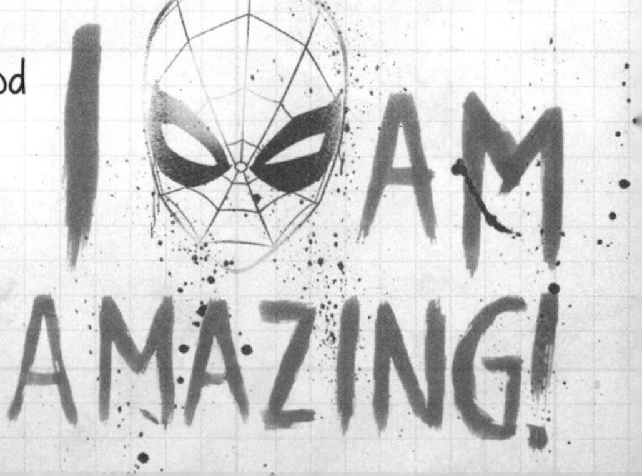
I AM
AMAZING!

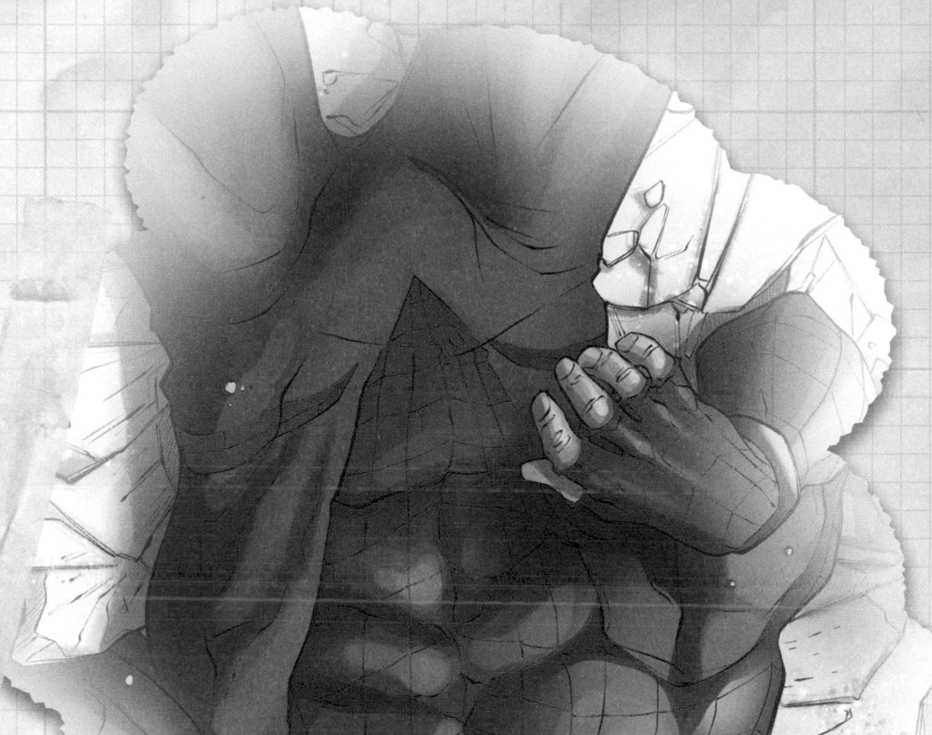

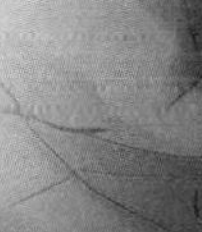

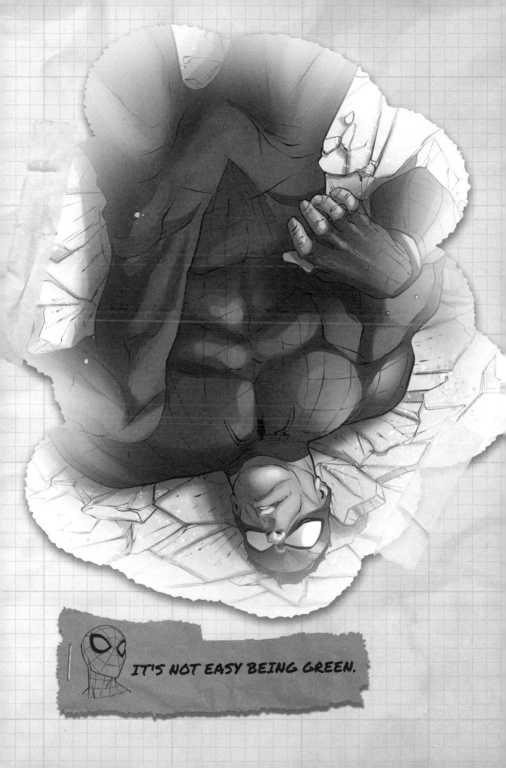

IT'S NOT EASY BEING GREEN.

Feeling like a Hulk-sized weight had been lifted off my shoulders, I thanked the doc and went to leave. He stopped me abruptly, claiming there was a lingering presence of negative energy in my dreamscape. So, it was best that he put me into another trance and do some more digging.

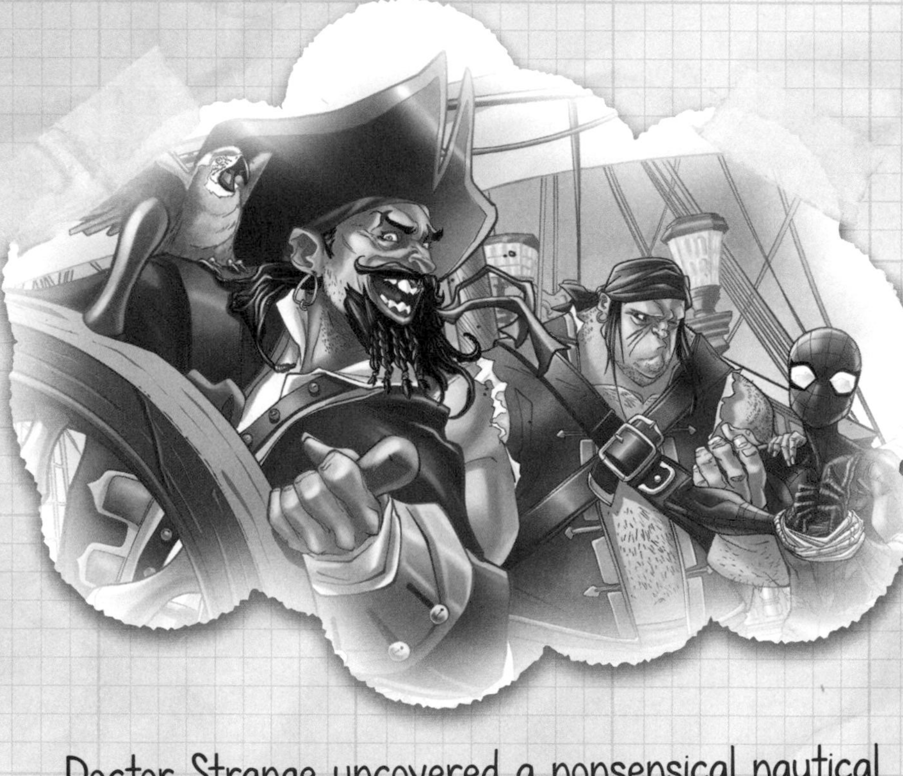

Doctor Strange uncovered a nonsensical nautical scene playing out across the high seas. Spider-Man had been captured by Blackbeard the pirate and forced to WALK THE PLANK to sleep with the fishes.

Dr. Strange snapped his fingers, waking me up. He had made a diabolical discovery. My fears and anxieties have increased because there is a frightening force haunting my dreamscape. It is none other than Doctor Strange's nocturnal nemesis—**NIGHTMARE!** (Certainly a fitting face to match the name.)

After being banished to another dimension by the Sorcerer Supreme long ago, Nightmare decided to exact his revenge by using MY brain as his battlefield.

Luckily, the doc had just the prescription for this pain...

Doctor Strange made a good old-fashioned house call and beamed a projection of himself into the astral plane where he faced off against his frightful foe.

Blasting the baddie back to the shadow realm with positive light energy, Doctor Strange cleared my mind and helped the nightmares stop.

Iron Man was right. There is no shame in asking others for help, and many a great victory is won using teamwork. Tony Stark has not only inspired me as a scientist and inventor, but as a slick super hero. Maybe it's time I started recruiting a ragtag team of my own.

JOURNAL ENTRY 12:

Get this. Today I met ANOTHER spider-powered teenager out there who is just like me! His name is Miles Morales and he, too, gained his abilities from a genetically altered spider.

We've become fast friends. What a relief to be able to share this blessing and curse with someone who understands exactly what it feels like. Miles even came up with his own marvelous moniker: **KID ARACHNID!**

Since Kid Arachnid was new to the whole Spider-hero game, I took him under my web and gave him a few pointers. After some web-slinging practice, we went out for burgers and shakes at this new place that opened up by the Central Park Zoo. But, when you're Peter Parker...trouble has a way of sniffing you out.

Truth be told, we still don't know why the R
stop to ask. We just knew we needed to stop h

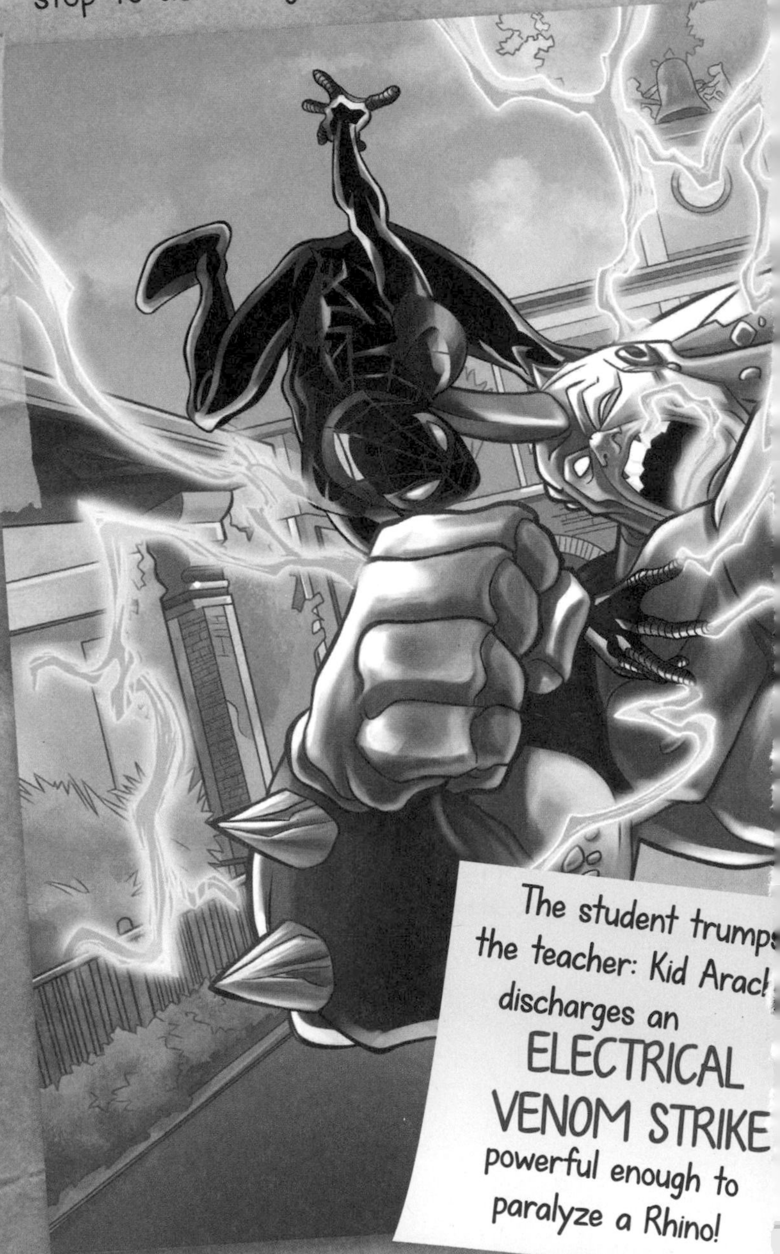

The student trumps
the teacher: Kid Arach
discharges an
ELECTRICAL
VENOM STRIKE
powerful enough to
paralyze a Rhino!

hino went on a rampage, and we didn't
im before he started a stampede.

nid

SPIDER-MAN AND HIS AMAZING ALLIES

CRIME FIGHTER

TEAM UP

MILES + SPIDEY

SPIDER-MEN?!

THREATS OR MENACES?

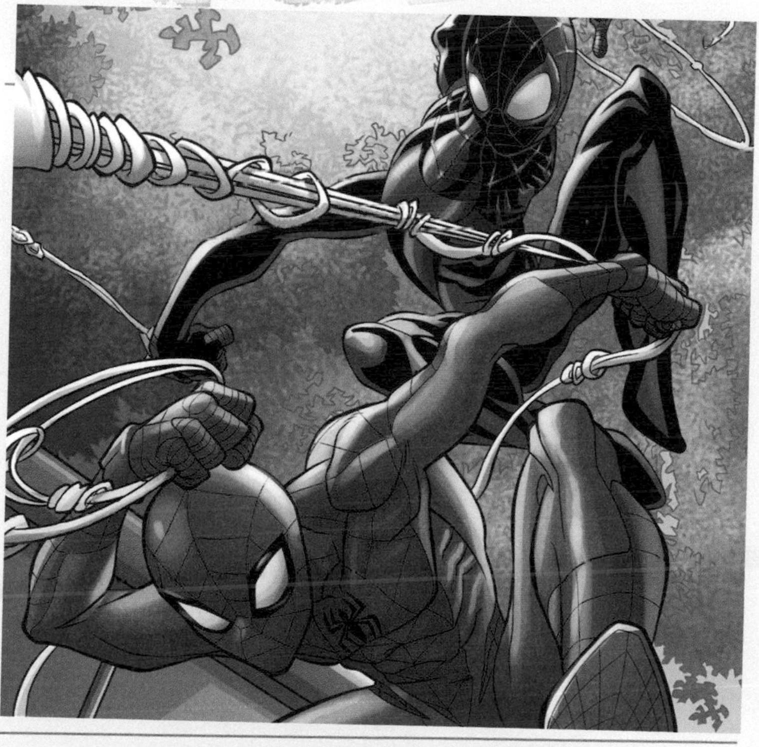

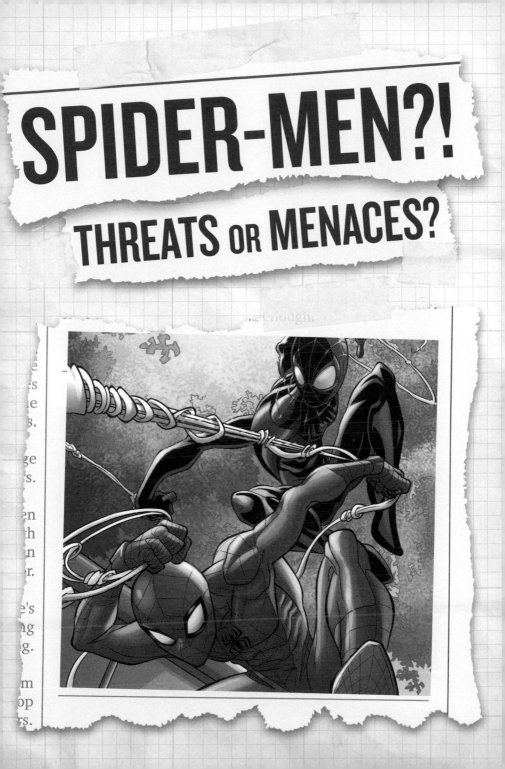

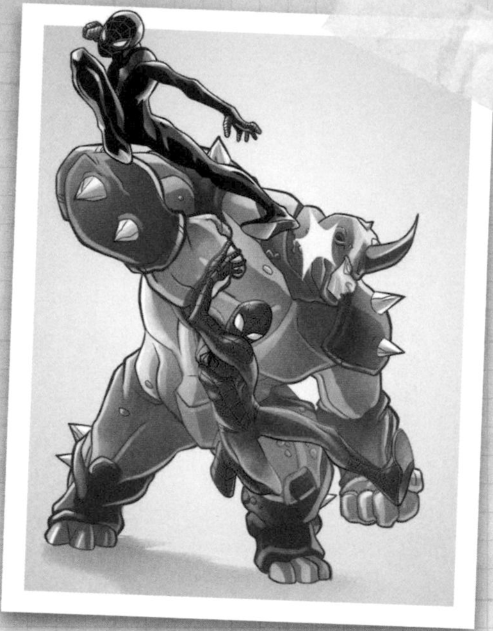

After a double dose of our terrific tag-team, Rhino became the zoo's newest exhibit and Miles and I finished our burgers and shakes...which were even better with the sweet smell of victory!

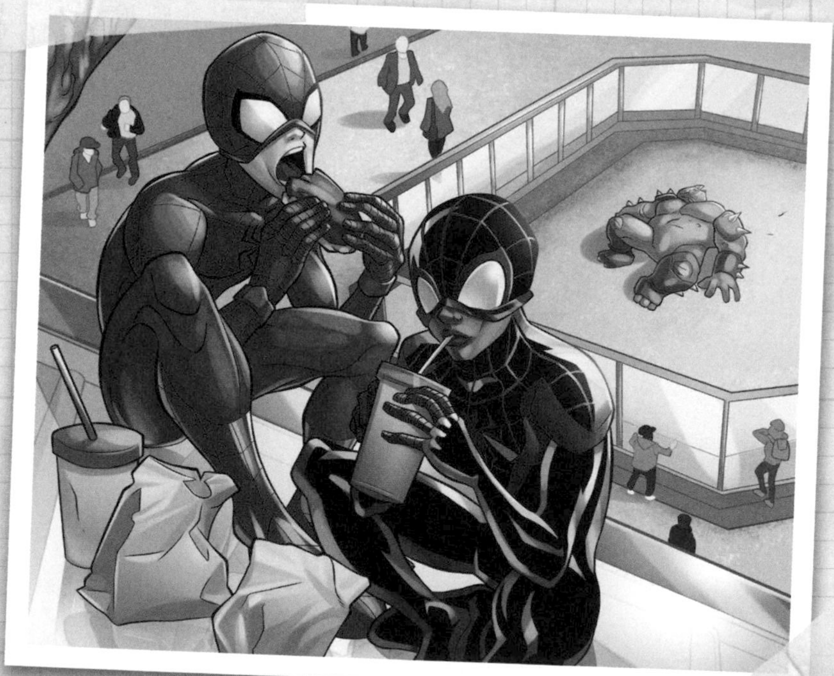

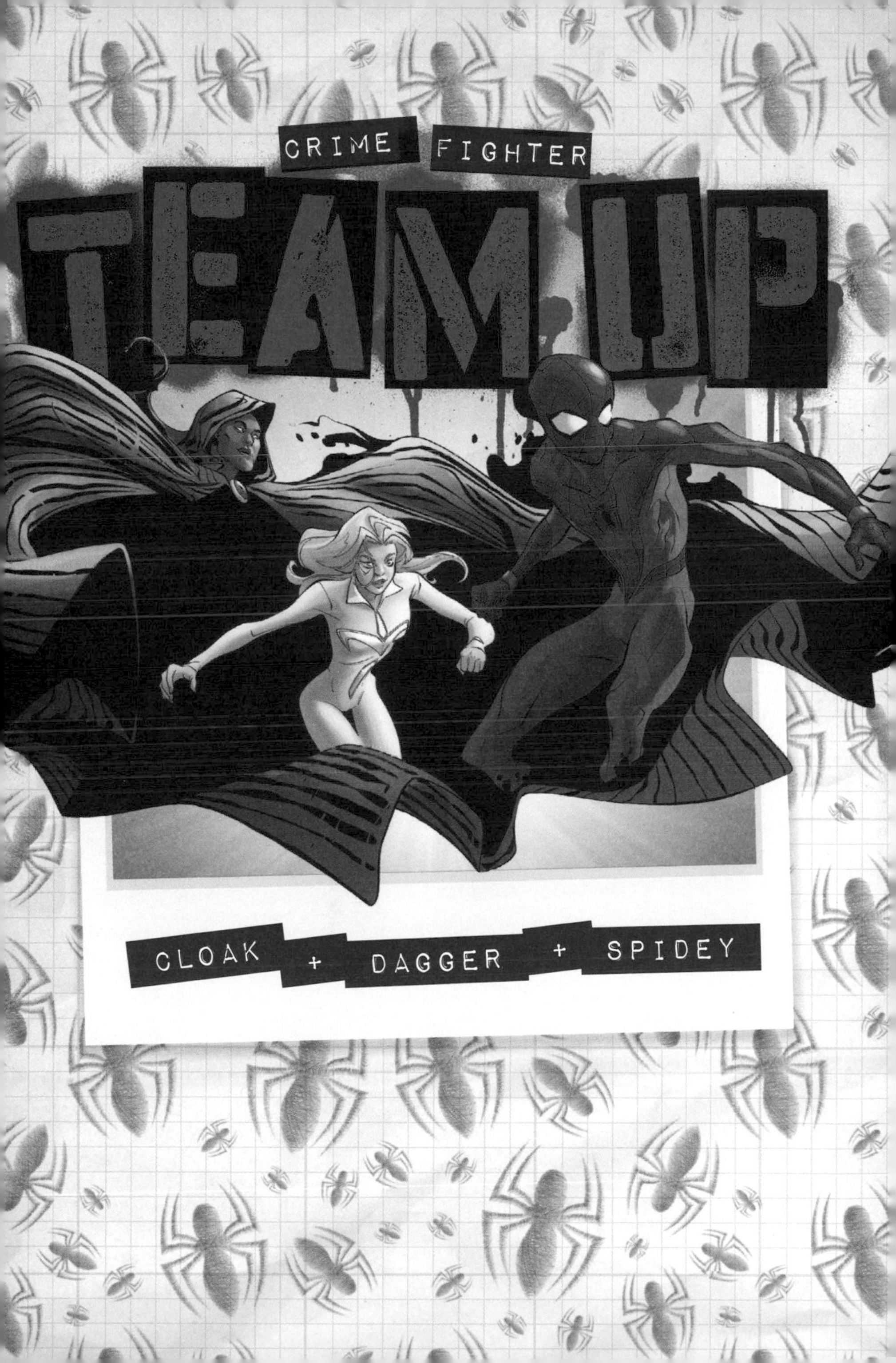
CRIME FIGHTER
TEAM UP
CLOAK + DAGGER + SPIDEY

JOURNAL ENTRY 13:

The last couple of days have been pretty quiet. It was a good thing for Spider-Man, since it gave him a break from breaking his back. It was a **bad** thing for Peter Parker, since he wasn't making money off of Spider-Man's daring deeds.

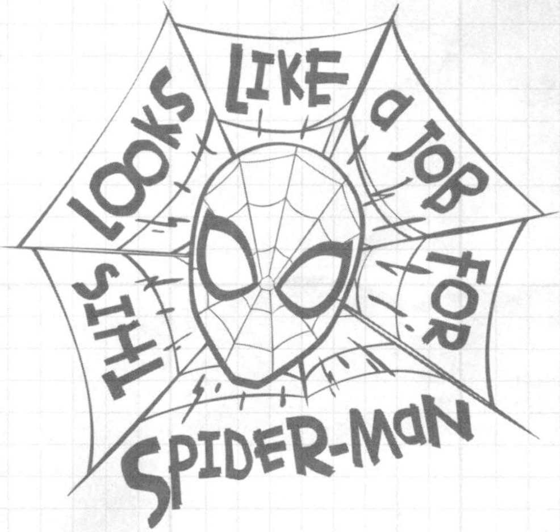
THIS LOOKS LIKE a JOB FOR
SPIDER-MAN

Feeling depressed, I asked Jameson to put me on other assignments and he threw a juicy missing persons case my way! We're not talking just regular missing—we're talking getting abducted by a supernatural force missing that leaves behind a magic residue.

Sign me up!

I created a little tracking device that guided me back from the scene of the crime to the Holy Ghost Church on 42nd street.

Once inside, I met the individuals responsible for the recent street-cleaning stunt:

CLOAK AND DAGGER!

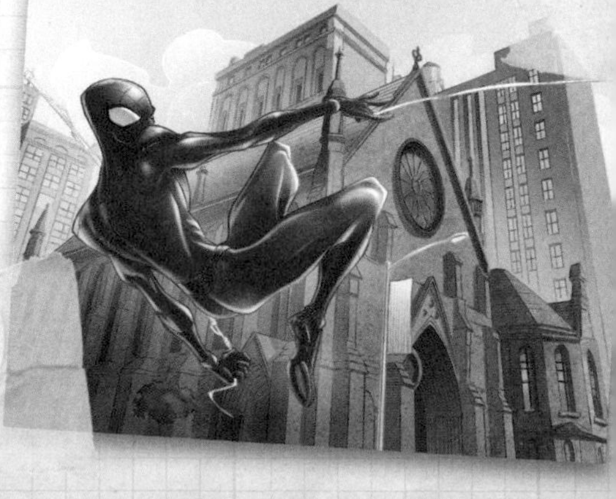

REAL NAME:
TYRONE JOHNSON

HEIGHT: 5'9"

WEIGHT: 155 LBS.

POWERS & ABILITIES

- ENHANCED STRENGTH AND INTANGIBILITY

- ABILITY TO MANIPULATE AND CREATE FIELDS OF DARKNESS

- CAN TELEPORT VIA THE DARKFORCE DIMENSION, A WORLD OF STRANGE EBONY ENERGY

CLOAK

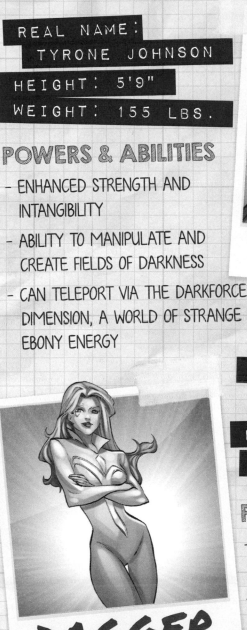

DAGGER

REAL NAME:
TANDY BOWEN

HEIGHT: 5'5"

WEIGHT: 116 LBS.

POWERS & ABILITIES

- GENERATES A FORM OF "LIVING LIGHT" CALLED THE LIGHTFORCE

- CAN CREATE AND THROW KNIVES MADE OF LIGHT FROM HER FINGERTIPS

- USES HER LIGHTFORCE ENERGY TO ILLUMINATE DARK AREAS

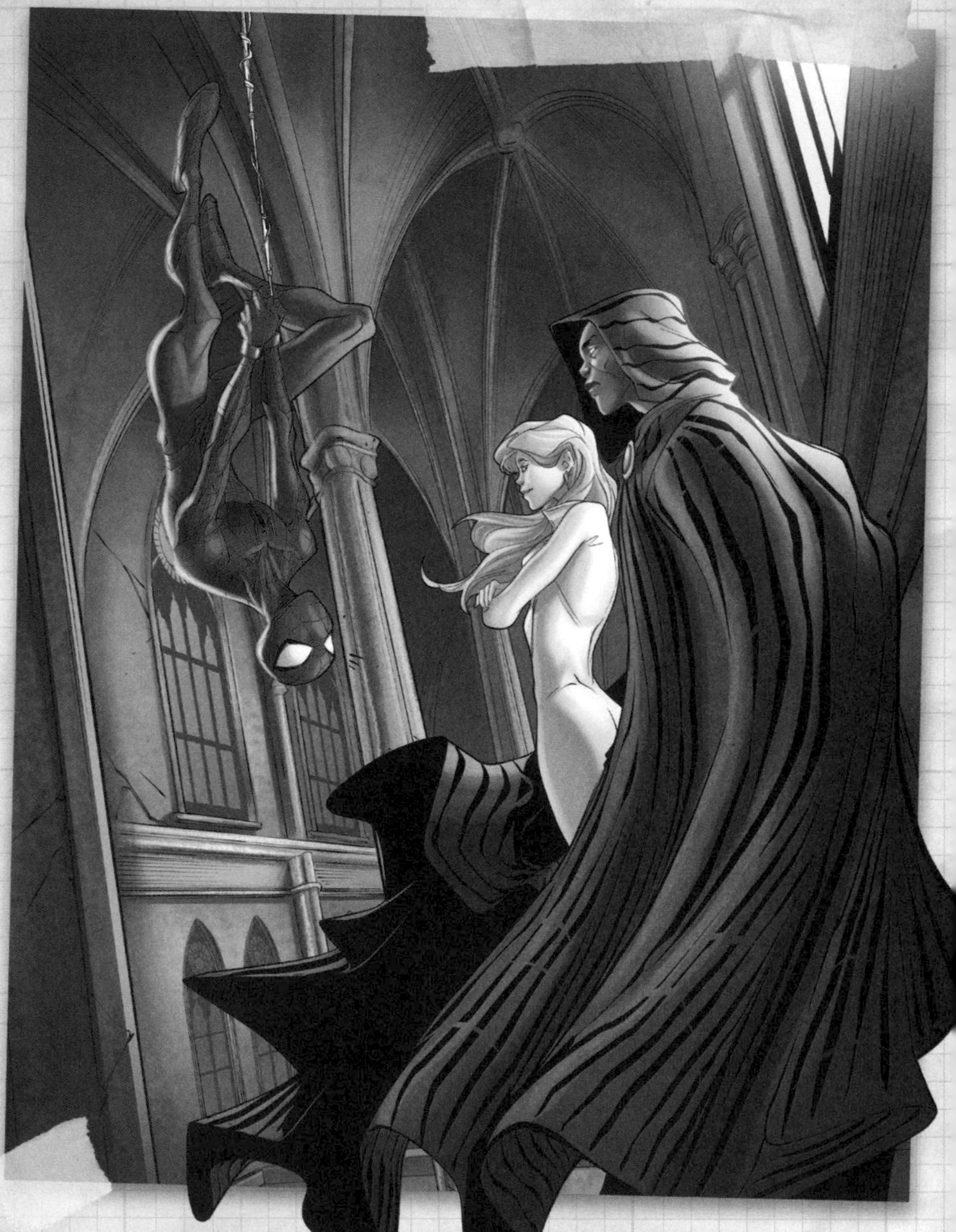

A combination of spooky and spunky, Tyrone and Tandy were really nice and down to earth. They had both escaped the mad scientists who used them as lab rats to test a new serum. The serum gave Cloak and Dagger supernatural powers, which they used against their captors! Dagger destroyed all traces of the toxin, while Cloak trapped their tormentors in the Darkforce Dimension.

Well, I guess that solves the missing persons mystery.

Cloak brought up a new case. He felt someone tapping into his teleportation force through multiple dimensions. Dagger added that they followed the mystery menace here until the track went cold.

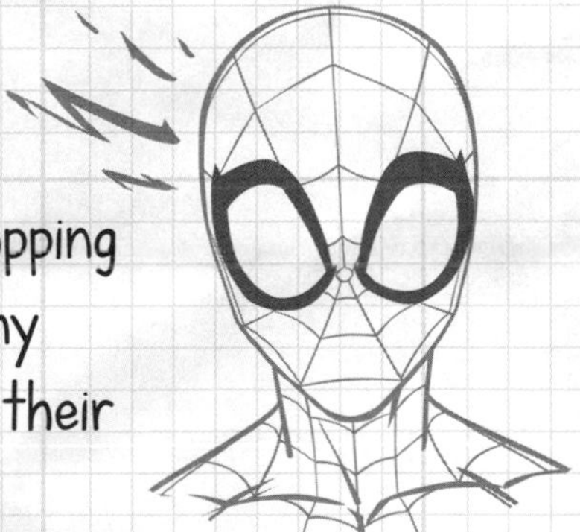

It felt like the universe was dropping another team-up adventure into my lap. Right when I offered to aid in their search, my Spider-Sense tingled!

Swinging out of the church, I saw my friend and classmate Gwen Stacy. Then I started seeing spots! Black circles appeared around Gwen...followed by disembodied hands snatching her purse. A polka-dotted head popped out and laughed!

SPOT had to be the teleporting entity Cloak and Dagger were looking for. I grabbed one of his hands, but the purse-snatcher sneered. He peeled off several of his polka-dots.

SEE SPOT RUN!

Then he proceeded to pummel me left and right by popping in and out of pocket dimensions. I felt like a piñata!

Just as quickly, Spot disappeared. Dagger rushed to my side and told me to hang on for the ride. Cloak pulled us into the Darkforce Dimension, where he traced Spot's teleportation force. In an instant, we materialized inside an abandoned warehouse...getting the drop on Spot!

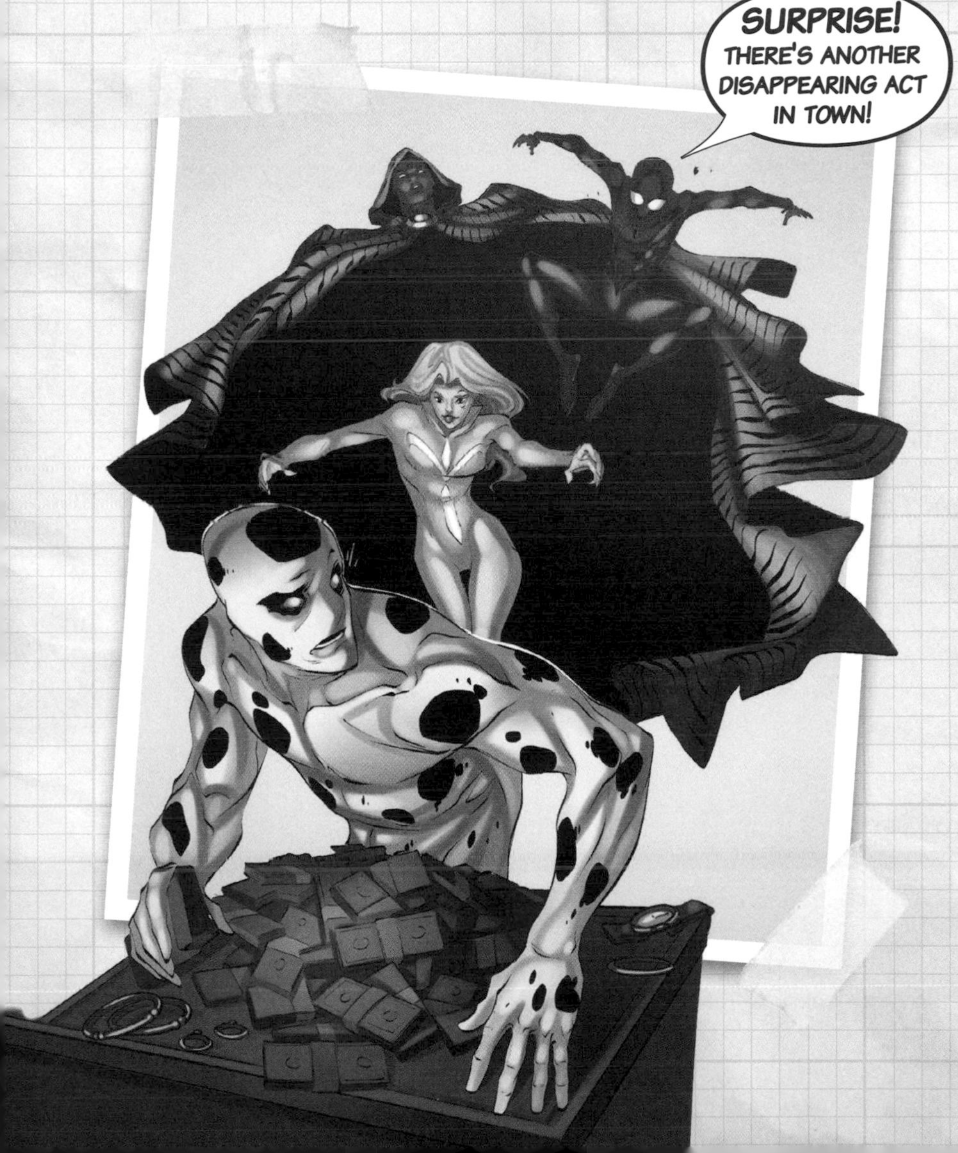
SURPRISE!
THERE'S ANOTHER DISAPPEARING ACT IN TOWN!

Spot's teleportation discs thrive on darkness, so he filled the room with them. In a flash, Dagger let loose a flurry of light knives. The brilliant bursts rendered Spot's powers inert and helped him see the error of his ways.

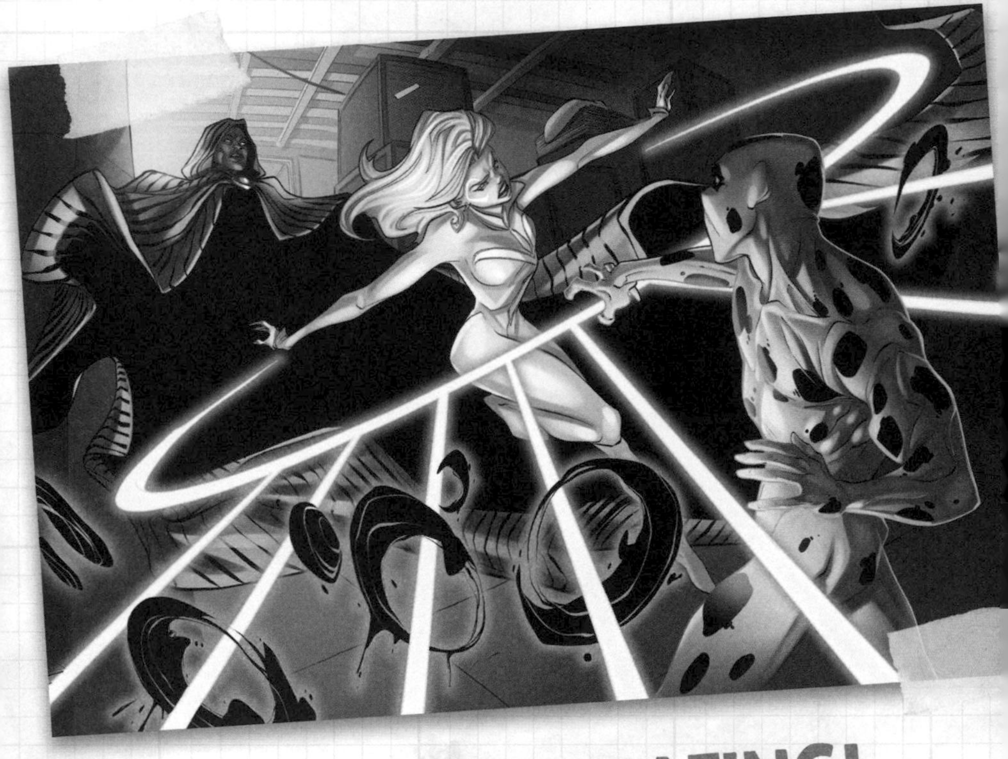

It was quite **ILLUMINATING!**

SEE WHAT I DID THERE..?

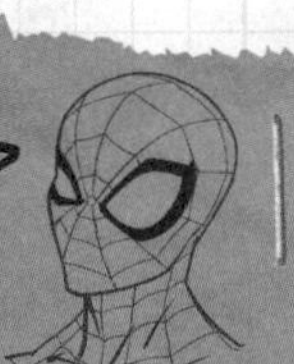

Finally, it was my turn to hop on Spot. Before he knew what hit him, I bundled him up in a cocoon of webbing. He was going nowhere fast. I spotted Gwen's purse and told Cloak and Dagger I'd return it to her.

The heroes thanked me for the assist and we exchanged contact info. Then Cloak whisked Dagger and Spot away.

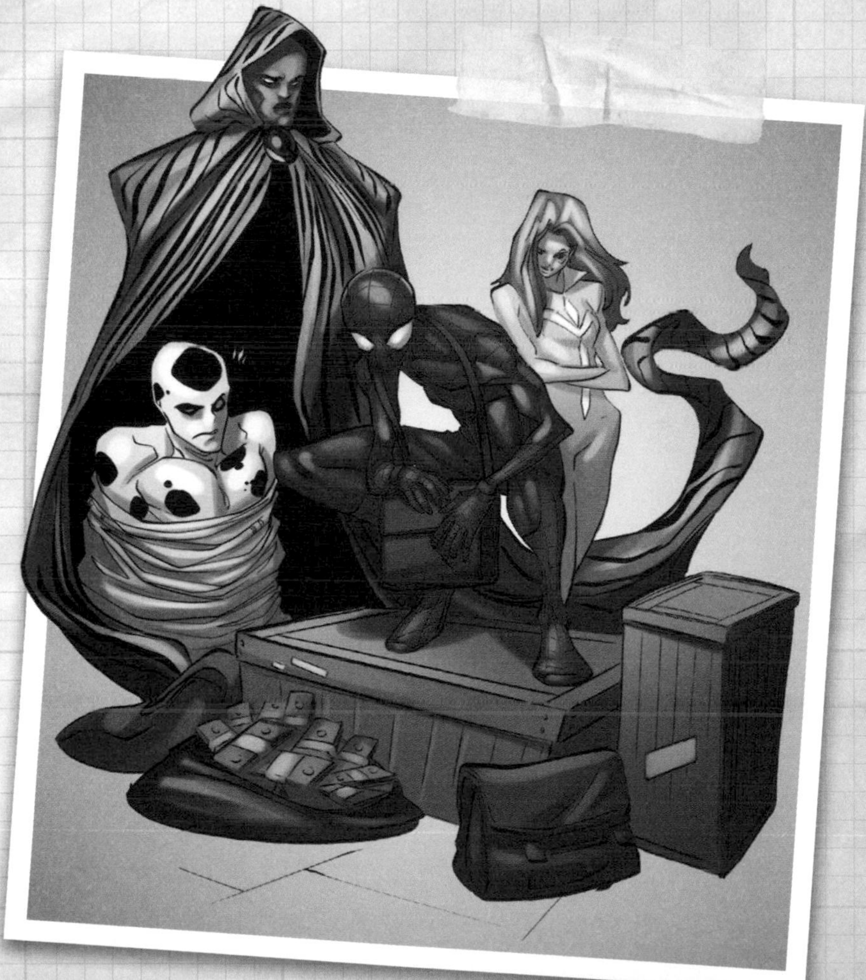

Quickly changing back into my street clothes, I found Gwen. She was pleasantly surprised when I told her that Spider-Man hooked me up with her purse after he caught the crook. Gwen treated us to hot dogs.

SCORE!

It was just what I needed to lift my spirits. My team-up with Cloak and Dagger reminded me that life has its rough spots, but there is always light in the darkness.

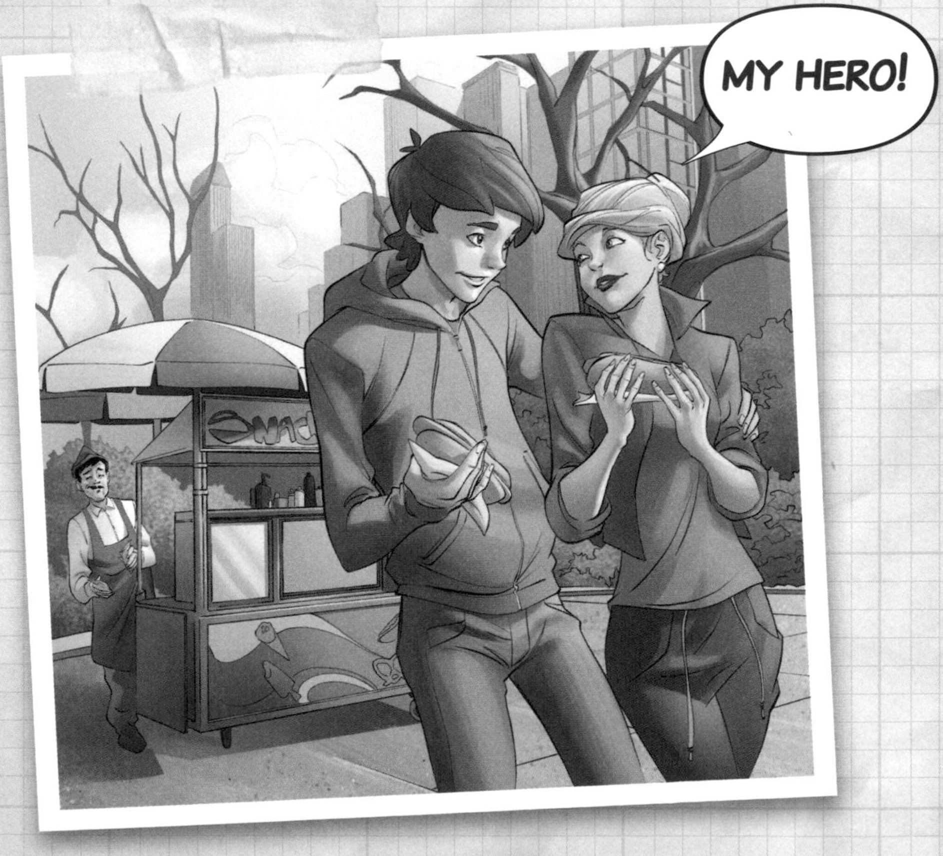
MY HERO!

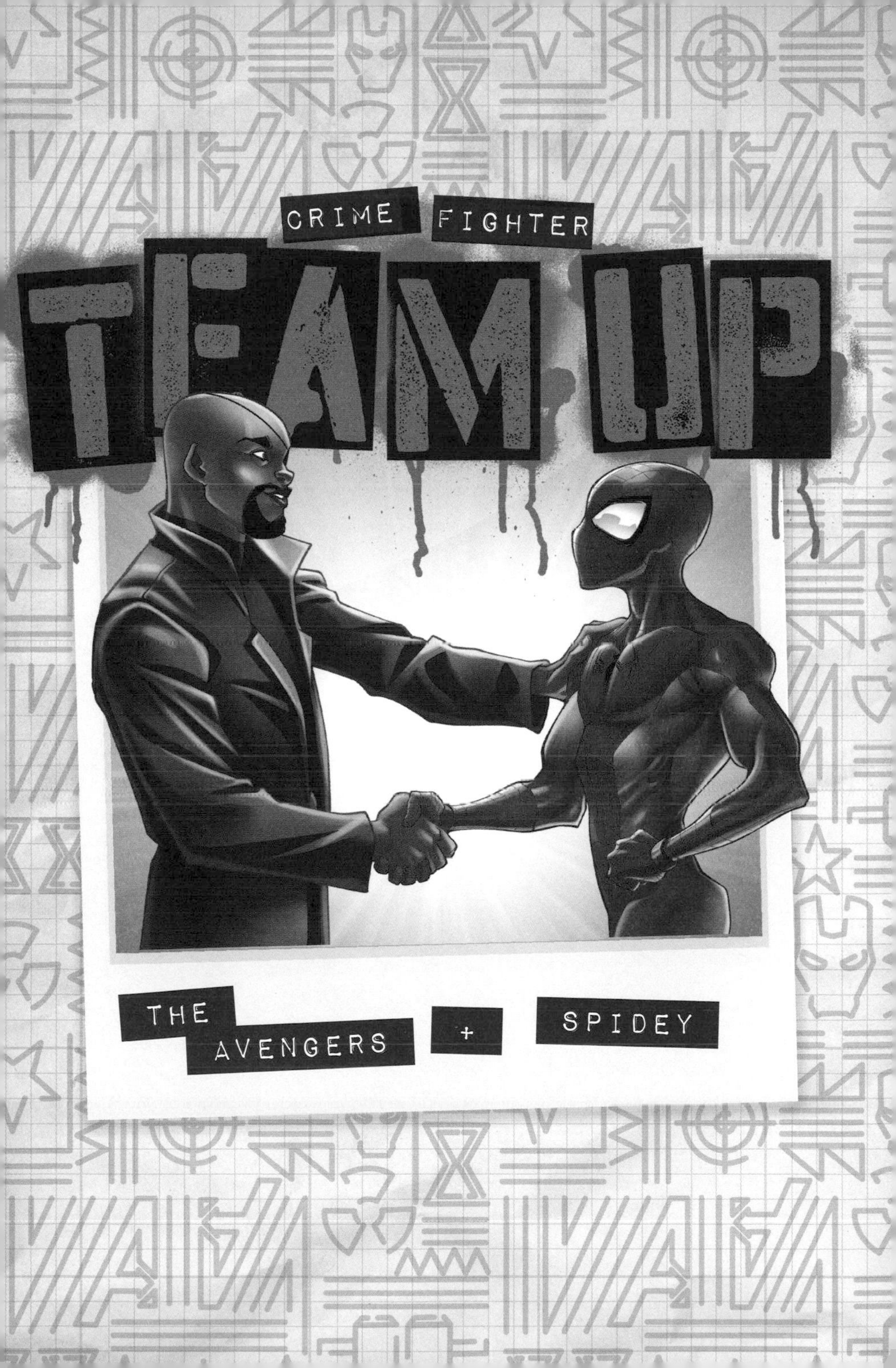
CRIME FIGHTER
TEAM UP
THE AVENGERS + SPIDEY

BEST. DAY. EVER!

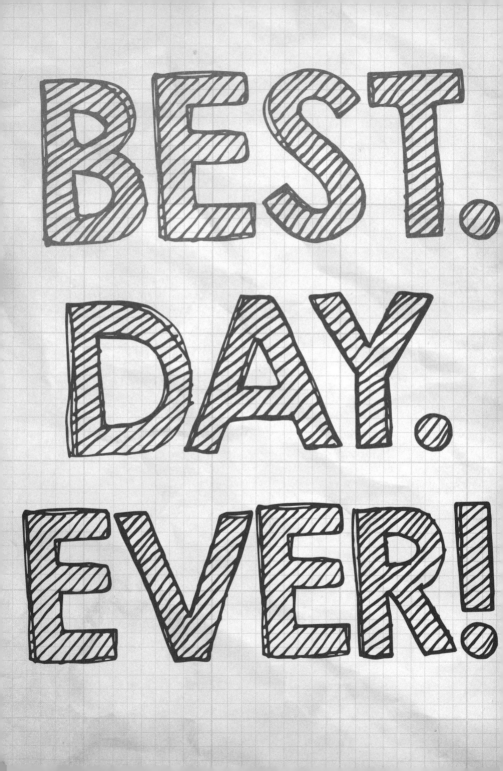

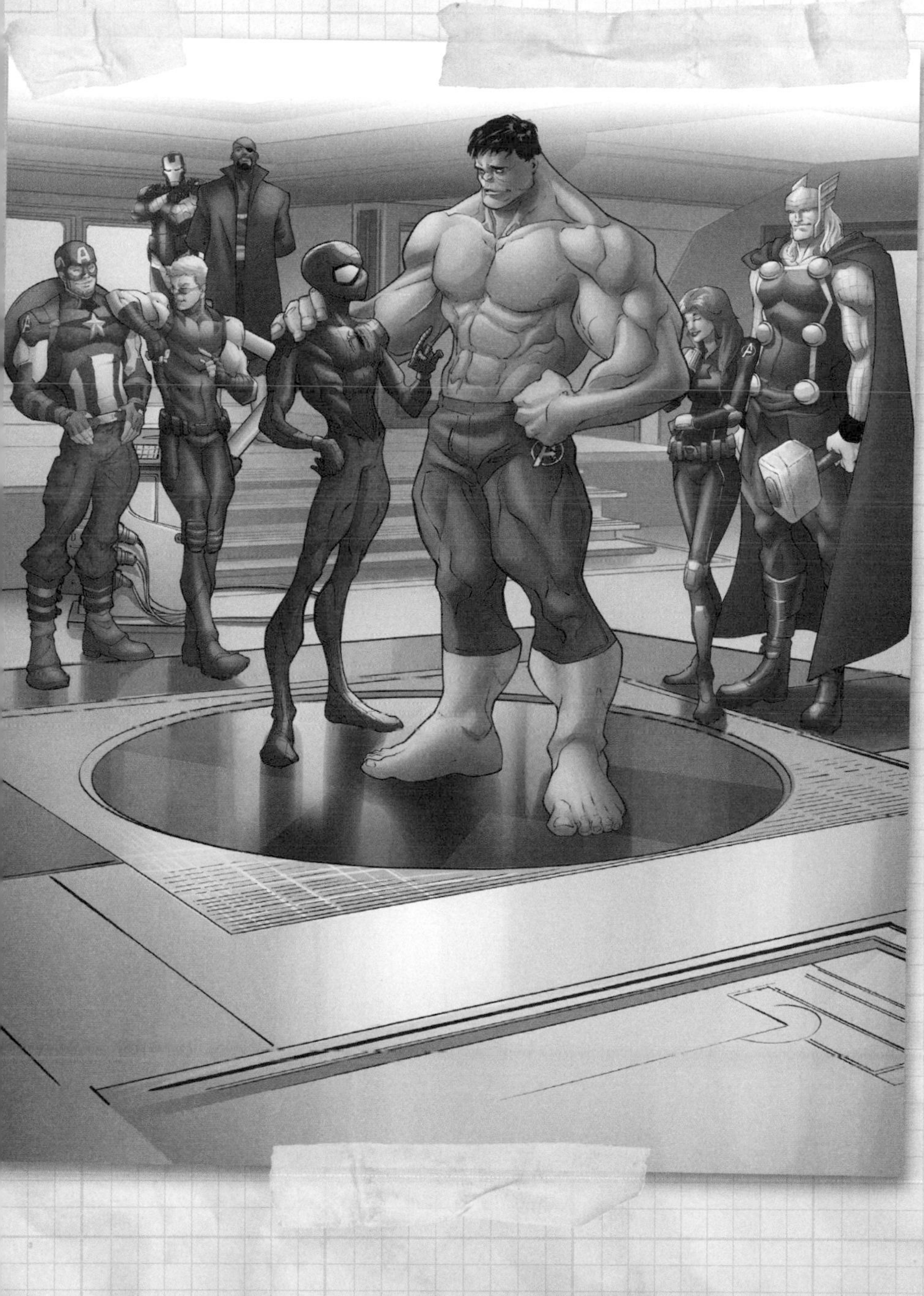

JOURNAL ENTRY 14:

Somebody pinch me! I can't believe what just happened is real. Meeting the Avengers in person? Pretty awesome. Fighting alongside them to save the world?

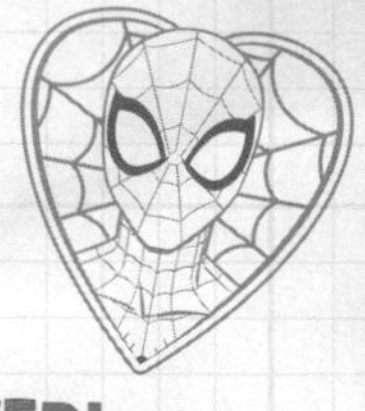

SQUAD GOALS ACHIEVED!

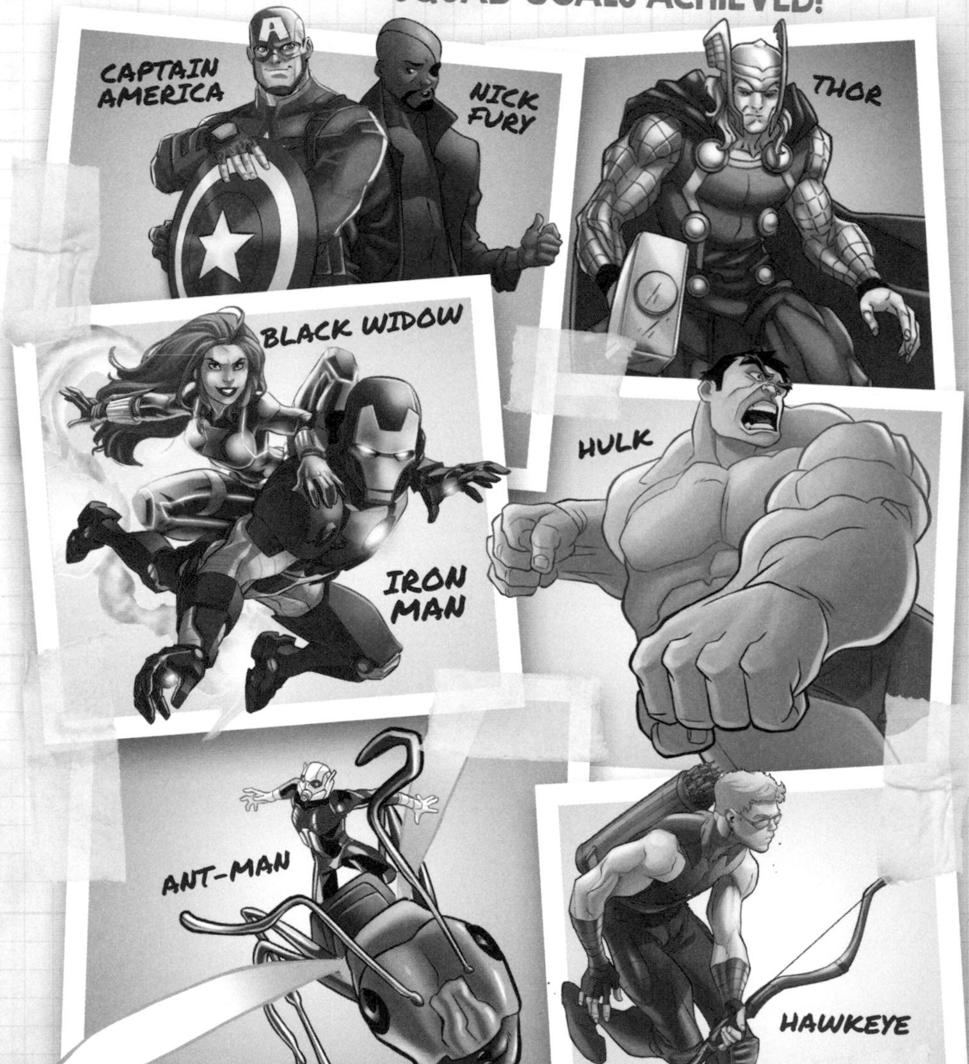
CAPTAIN AMERICA
NICK FURY
THOR
BLACK WIDOW
IRON MAN
HULK
ANT-MAN
HAWKEYE

I'm basically besties with the Earth's Mightiest Heroes. **NBD.**

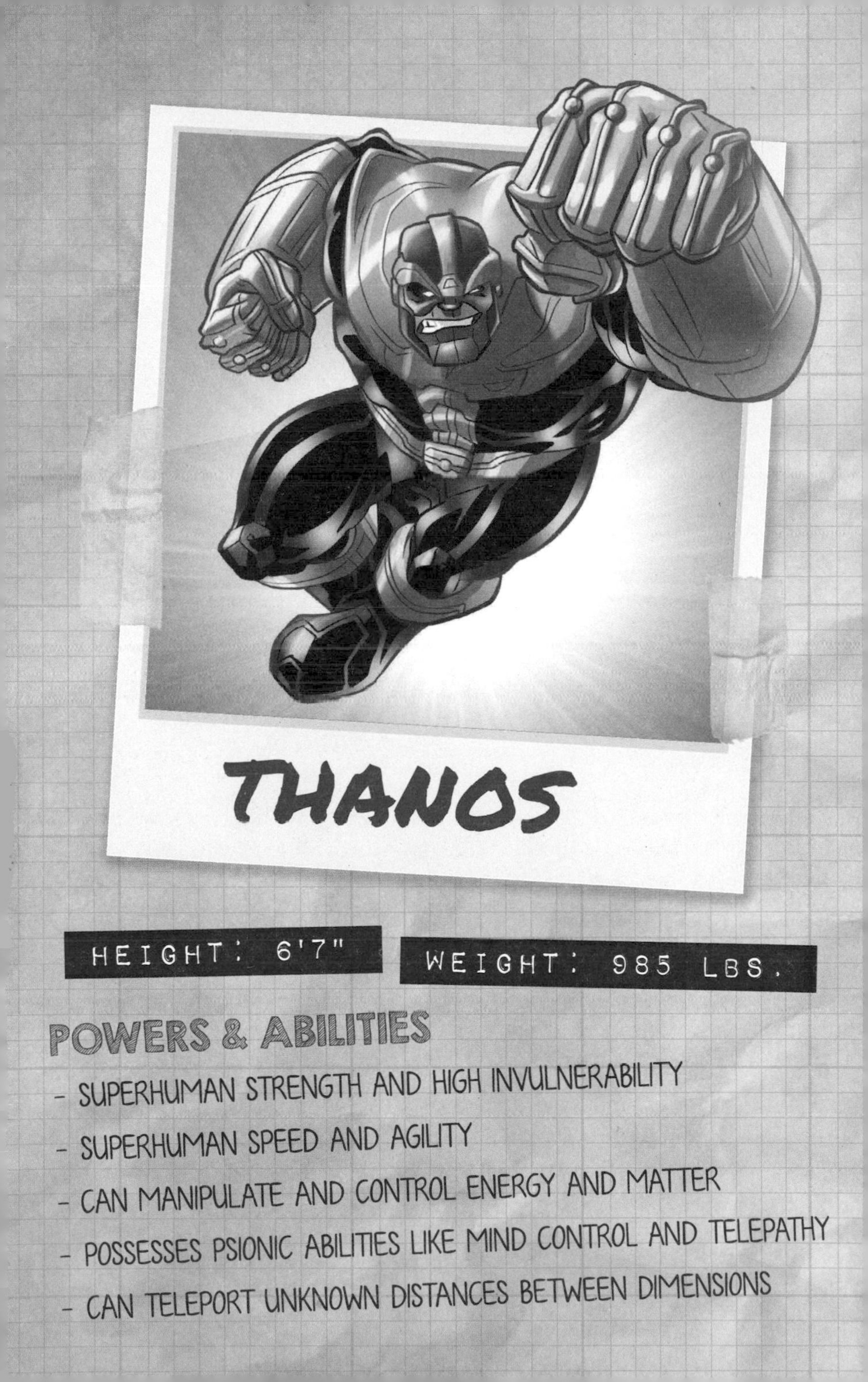

THANOS

HEIGHT: 6'7"

WEIGHT: 985 LBS.

POWERS & ABILITIES

- SUPERHUMAN STRENGTH AND HIGH INVULNERABILITY
- SUPERHUMAN SPEED AND AGILITY
- CAN MANIPULATE AND CONTROL ENERGY AND MATTER
- POSSESSES PSIONIC ABILITIES LIKE MIND CONTROL AND TELEPATHY
- CAN TELEPORT UNKNOWN DISTANCES BETWEEN DIMENSIONS

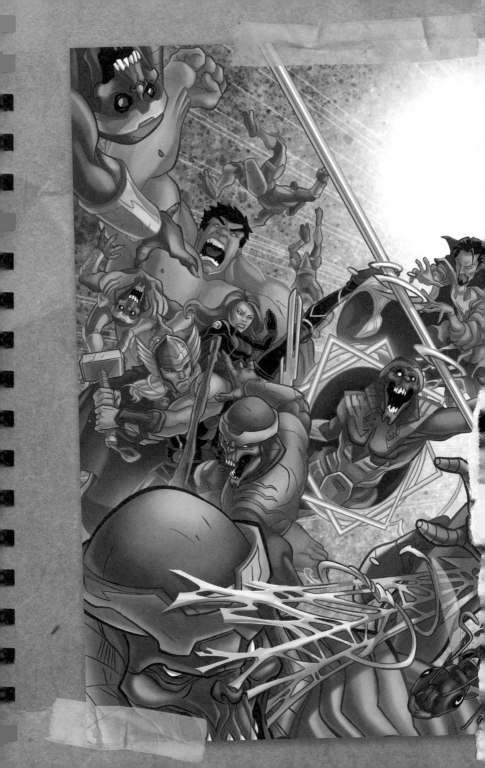

Cap isn't the only guy who can call a team together.
I brought my own amazing friends to the party!

When the intergalactic conqueror **THANOS** and his army of alien cyborgs—known as the Chitauri—attacked, Cap called for all available heroes to help.

That included your friendly neighborhood Spider-Man... **ME!**

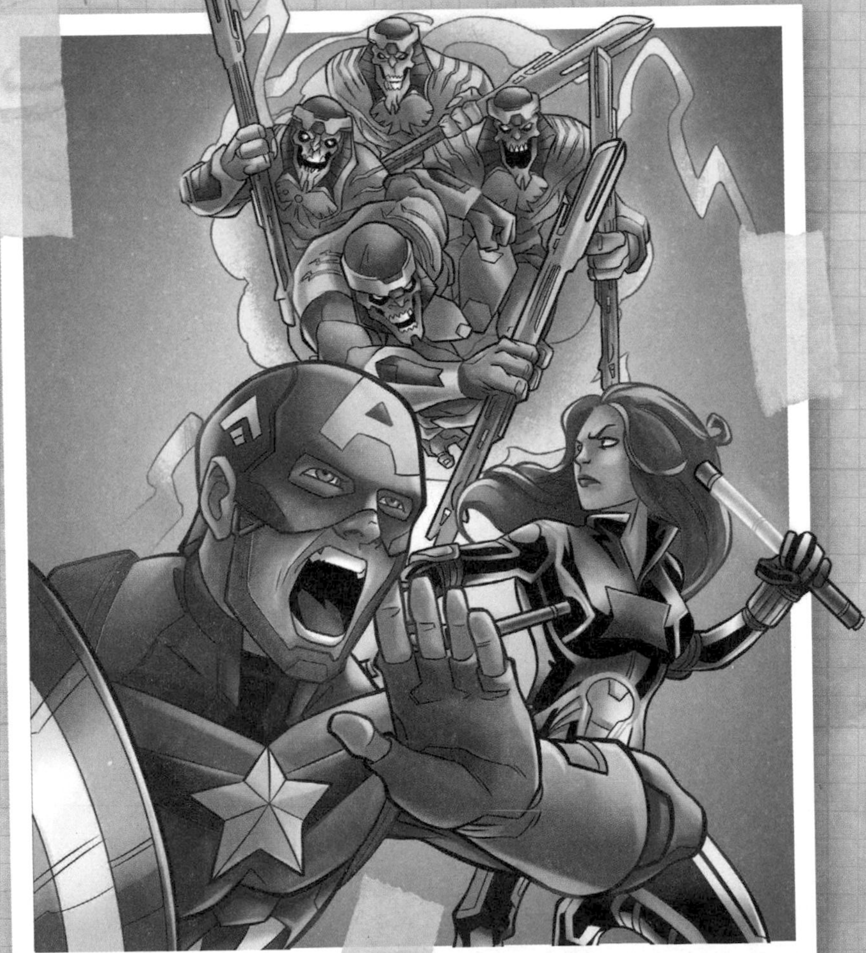

As the terrific team trashed the terrible Titan, my Spider-Sense tingled again. Trouble was brewing near Times Square...and it wasn't just those clowns dressed as Iron Man tricking tourists into taking pictures with them.

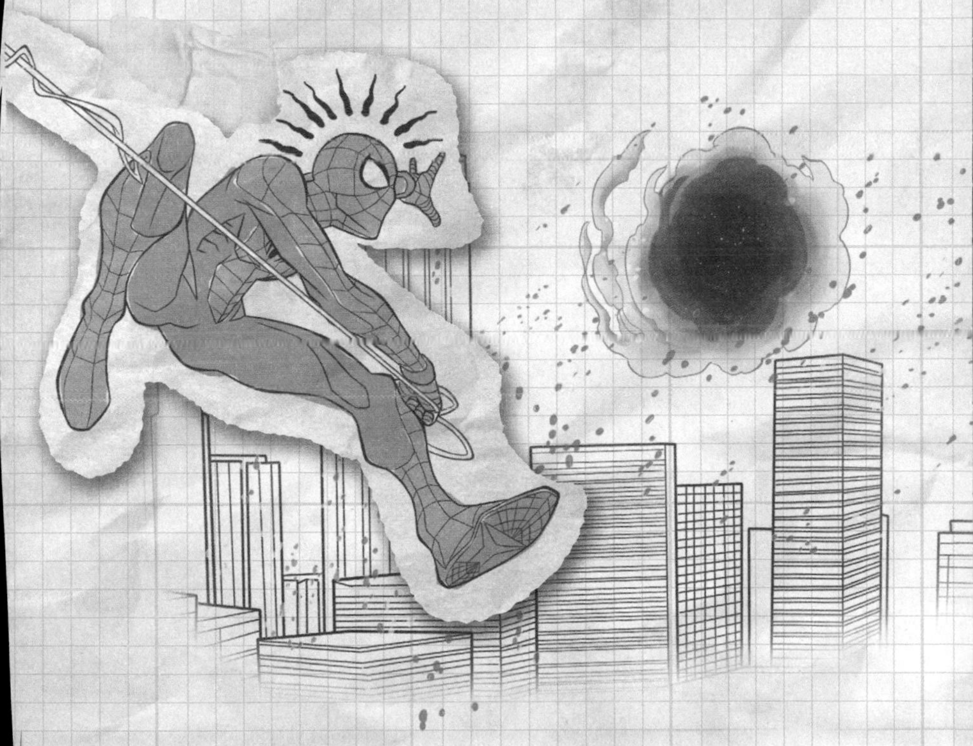

Another perilous portal opened and I needed to swing downtown and thwart the threat!

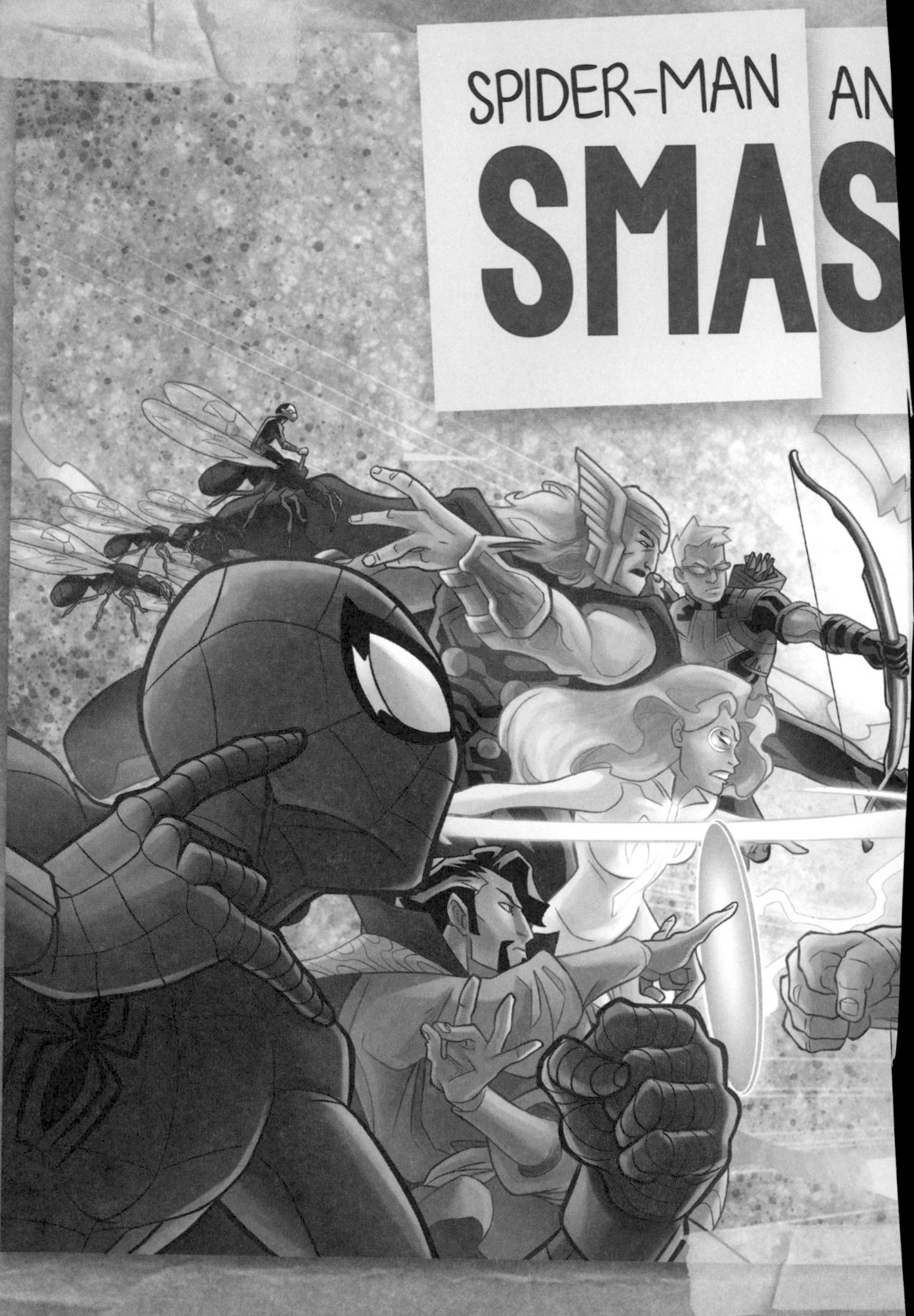
SPIDER-MAN AN
SMAS

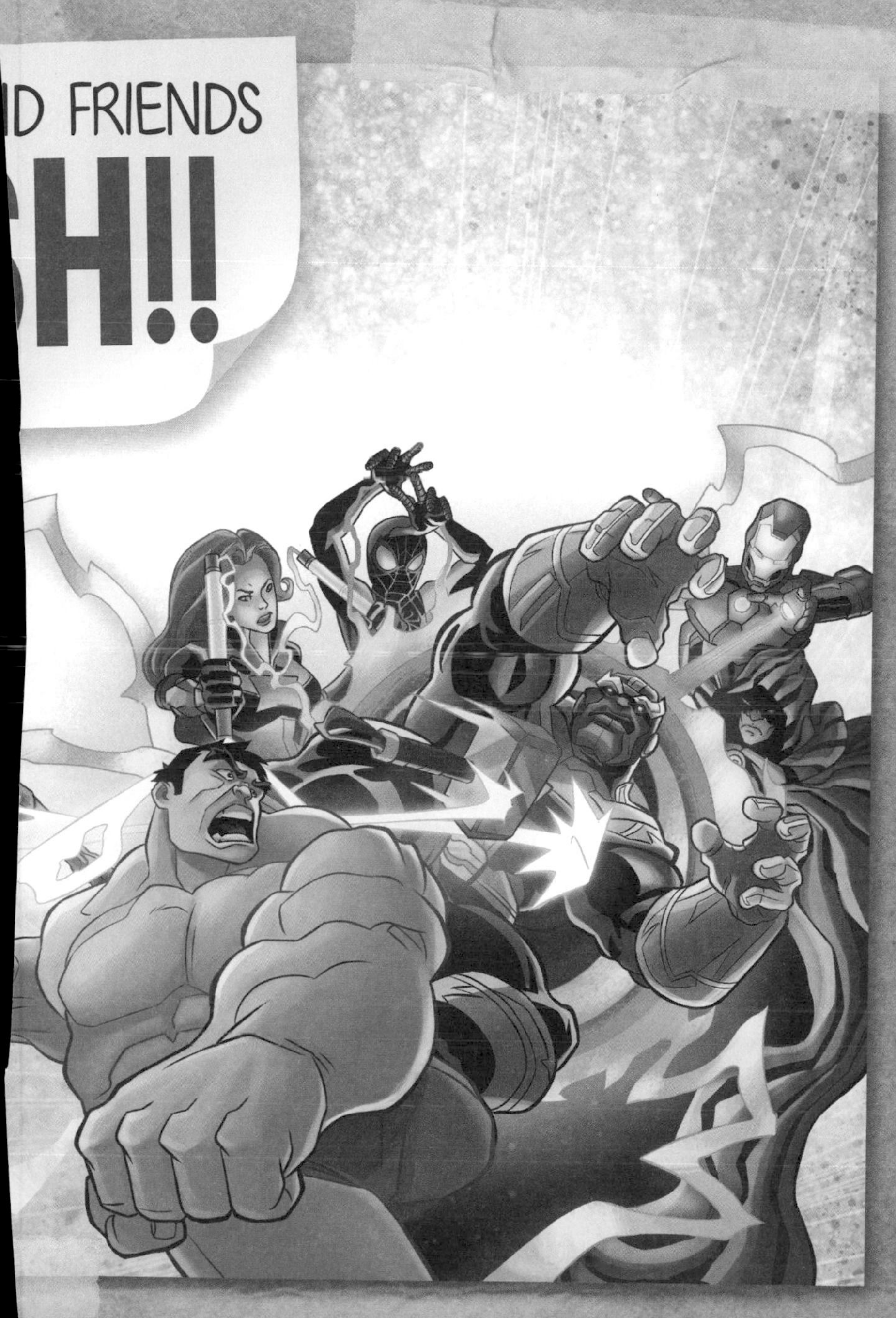

ND FRIENDS
SH!!

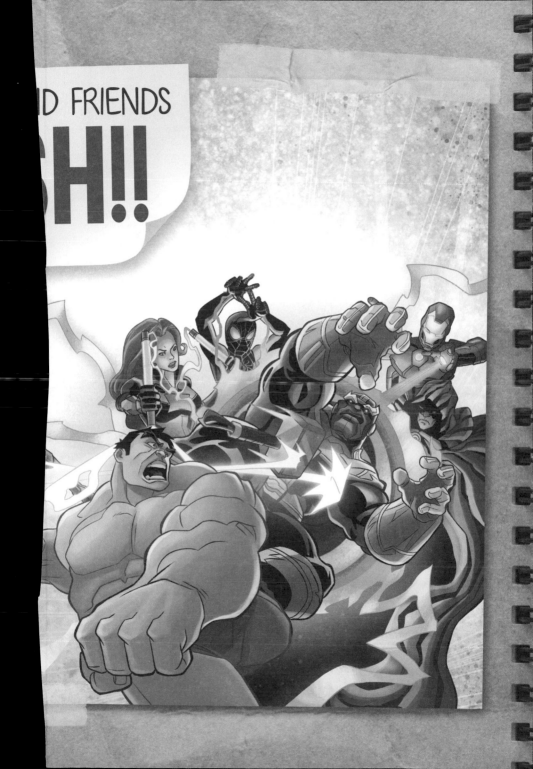

The fight was fierce but the Chitauri were chumps. I even joked about how Thanos should show his **BIG UGLY FACE** so we can kick his **BIG UGLY BUTT** back to space.

Then my Spider-Sense tingled.

He was right behind me.
Me and my big mouth, that is!

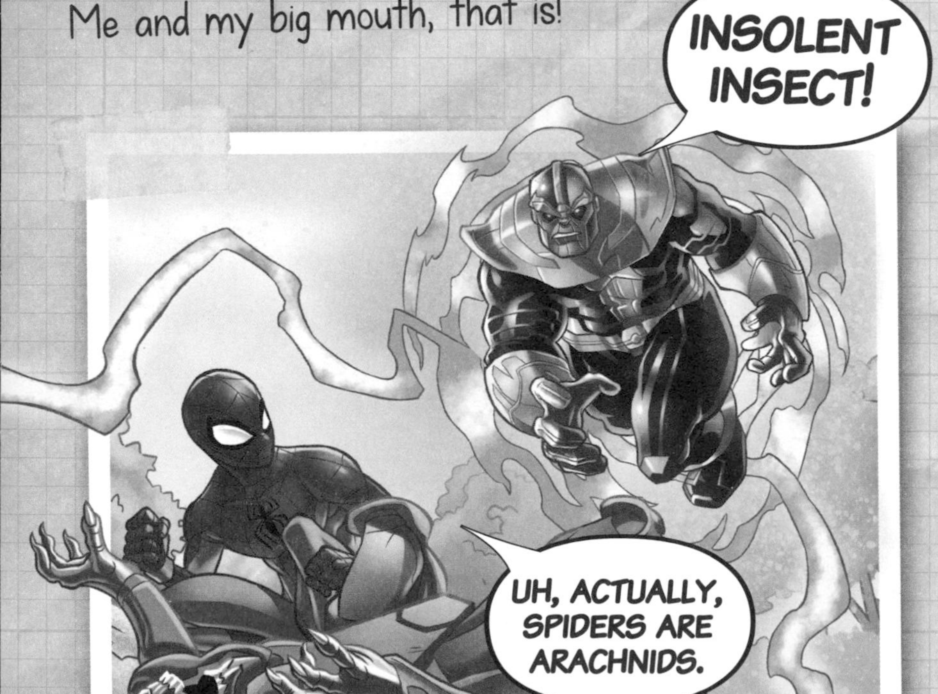
INSOLENT INSECT!
UH, ACTUALLY, SPIDERS ARE ARACHNIDS.

The warm sunshine suddenly turned into a cold blizzard. The source of the climate change was Thor's bad news brother—**LOKI!** That troublesome trickster had intercepted the Cosmic Cube from Thanos and was using it in his own sinister scheme to take over Earth. Can't these guys find another hobby?

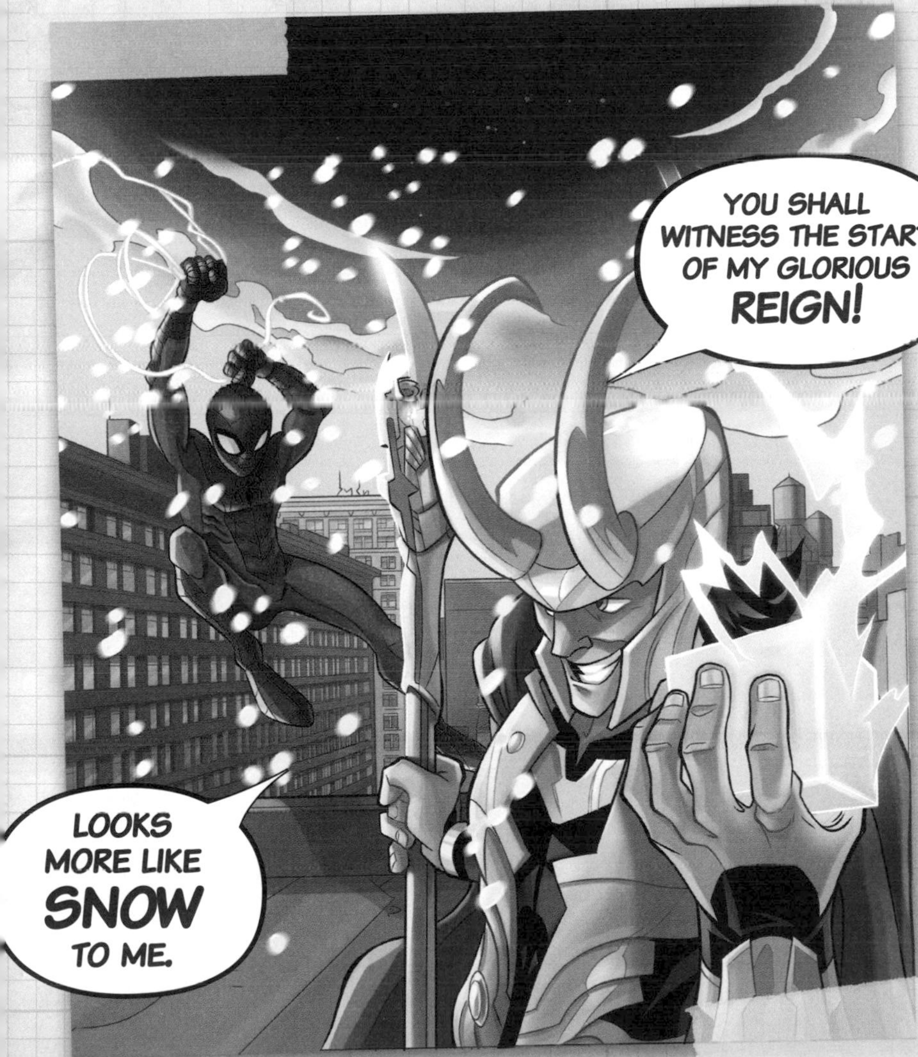
YOU SHALL WITNESS THE START OF MY GLORIOUS REIGN!
LOOKS MORE LIKE SNOW TO ME.

I was confident I could take Loki in a physical fight, but less so about the three hulking **FROST GIANTS** barreling through the portal straight at me! It's never fluffy kittens or cute puppies, is it?

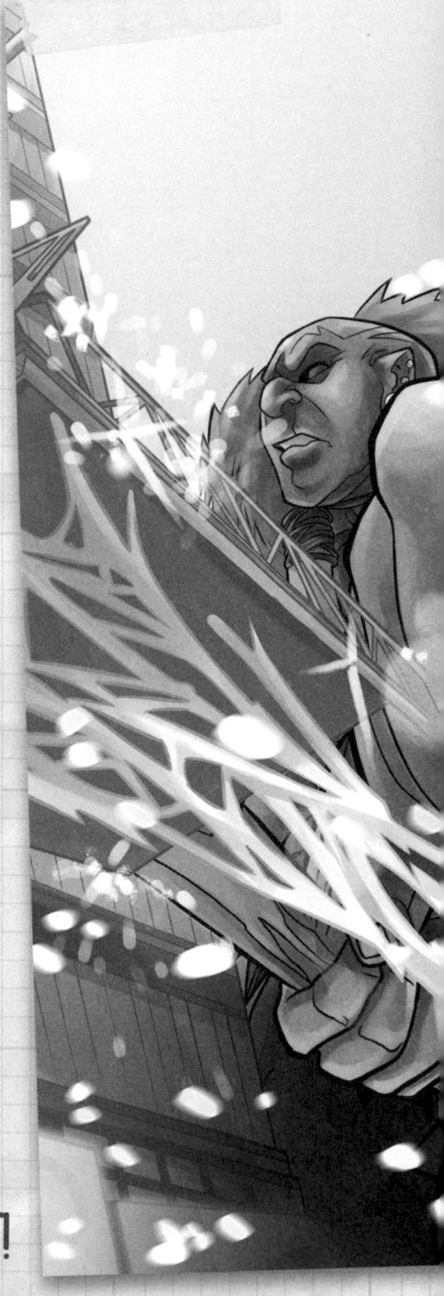

Thinking quickly, I sprayed as much web fluid as I could to create a barrier between two billboards. It bought me some time, but I needed a plan...

AND I NEEDED IT FAST!

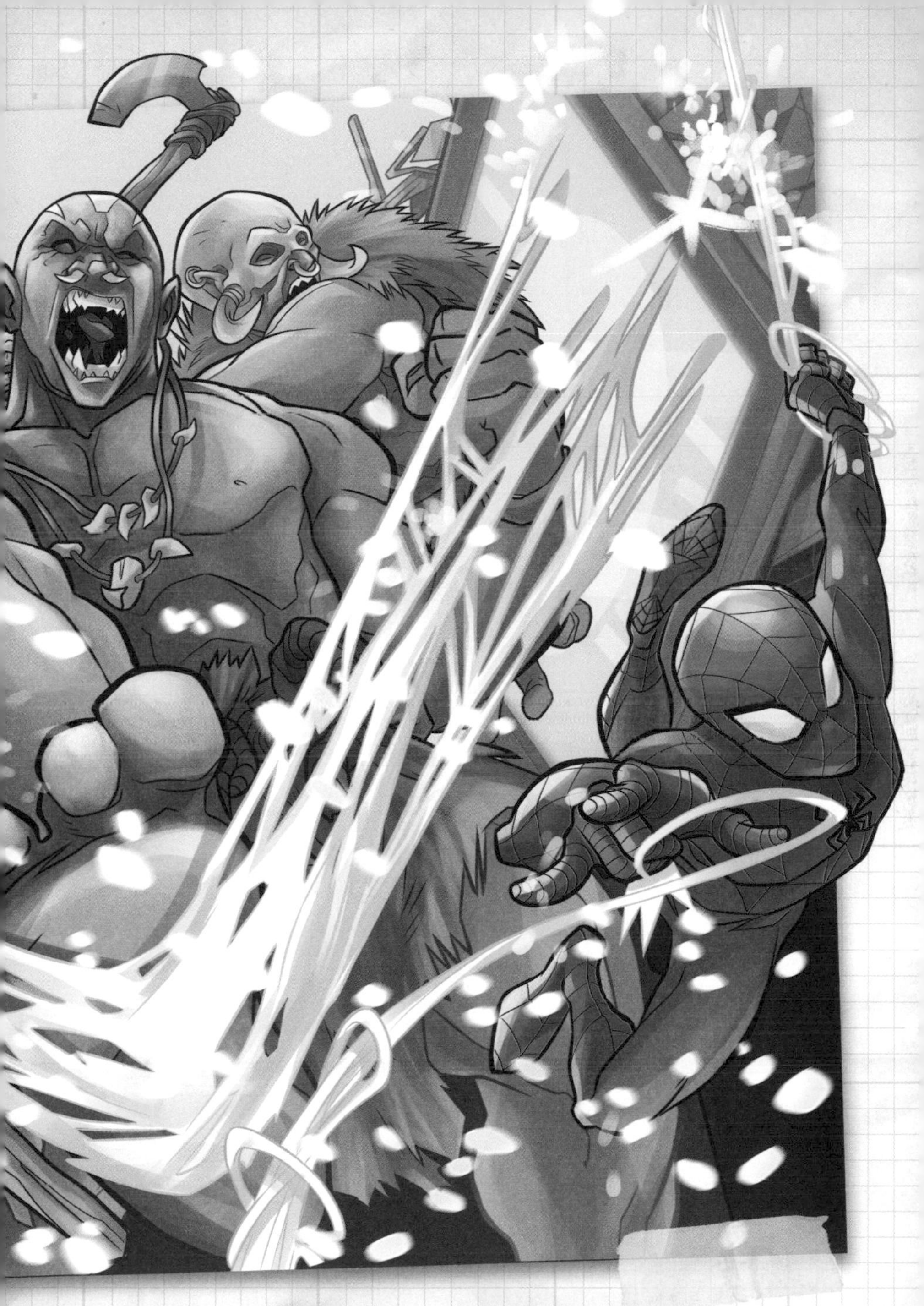

Talk about luck! The Quinjet appeared overhead. It was then that I knew the Avengers would have my back. They were going to send in the big guns and these Frost Giants were going to get crushed into ice cubes!

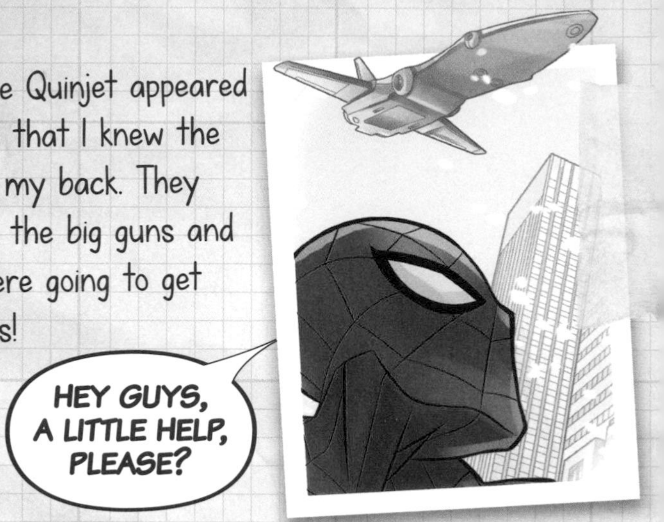
HEY GUYS, A LITTLE HELP, PLEASE?

Or so I thought. Imagine my dismay when only one Avenger disembarked. I mean, beggars can't be choosers, but did it have to be **ANT-MAN?**

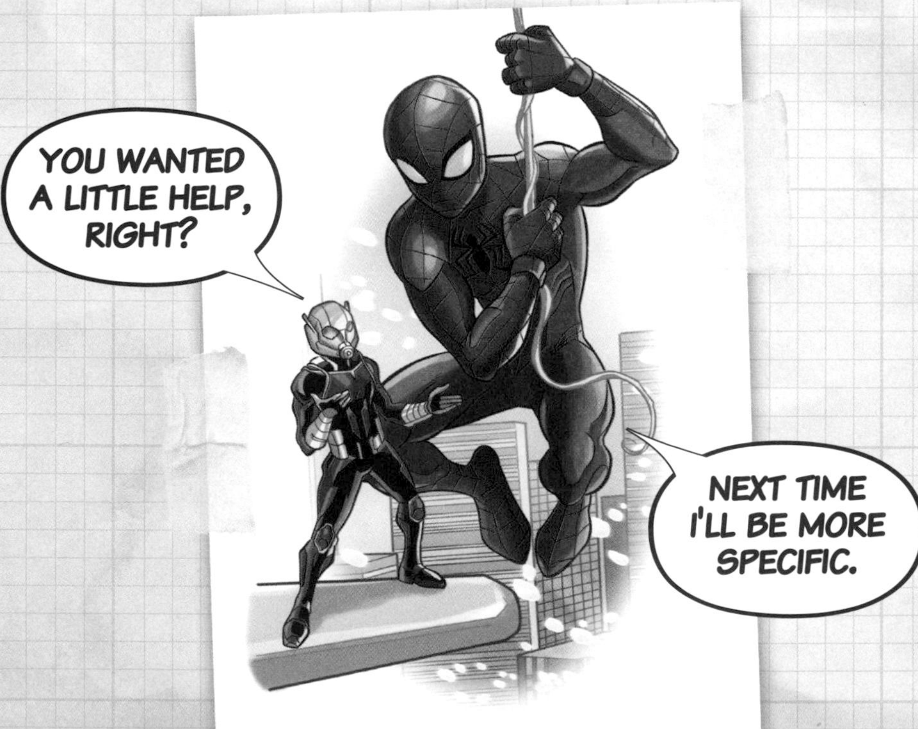
YOU WANTED A LITTLE HELP, RIGHT?
NEXT TIME I'LL BE MORE SPECIFIC.

While the city's super heroes thrashed Thanos, these bug-buddies played hard to get.

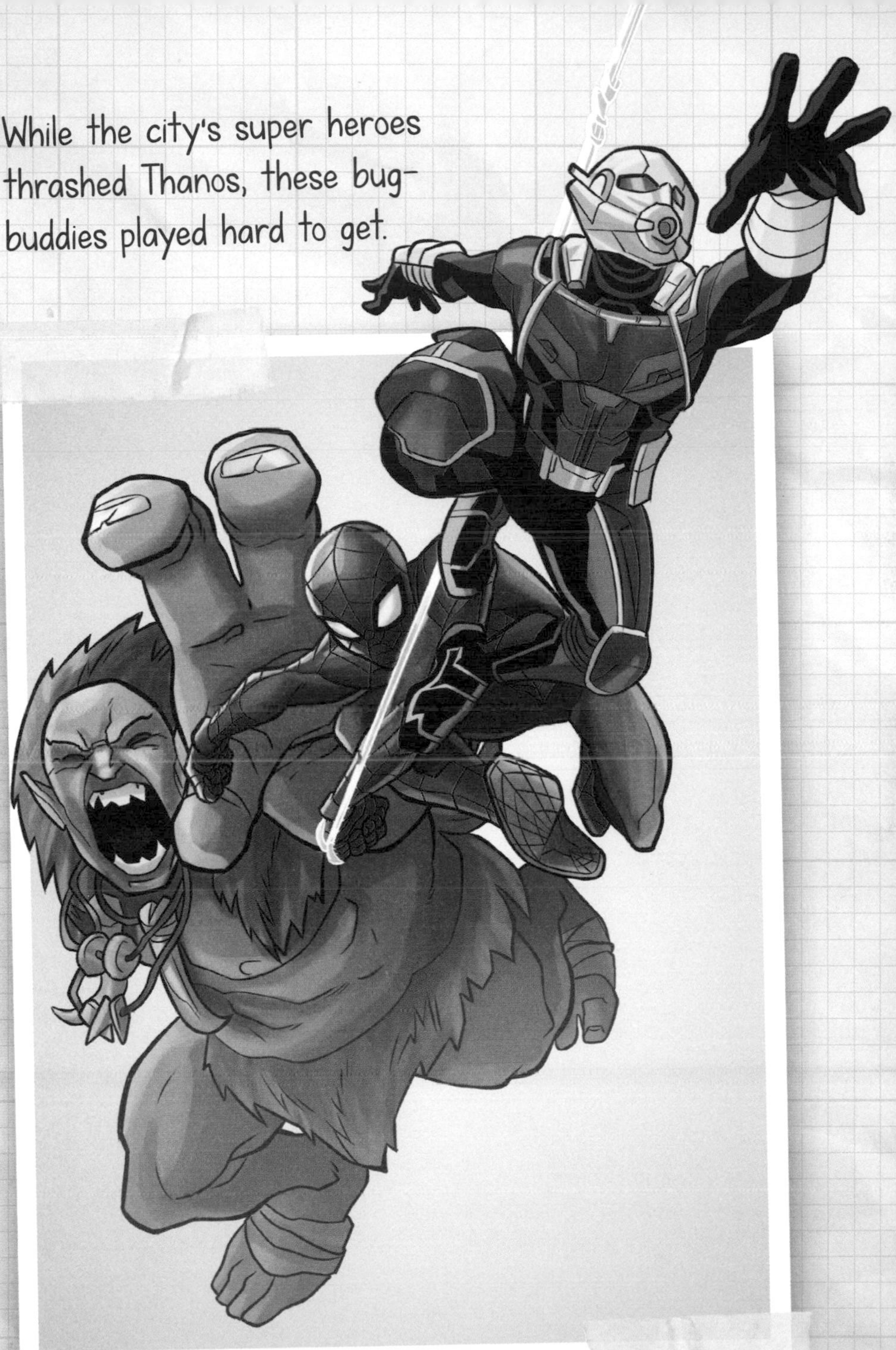

Together, Ant-Man and I came up with a bright idea: Use real-world science for an otherworldly opponent. We were going to bring the **HEAT!**

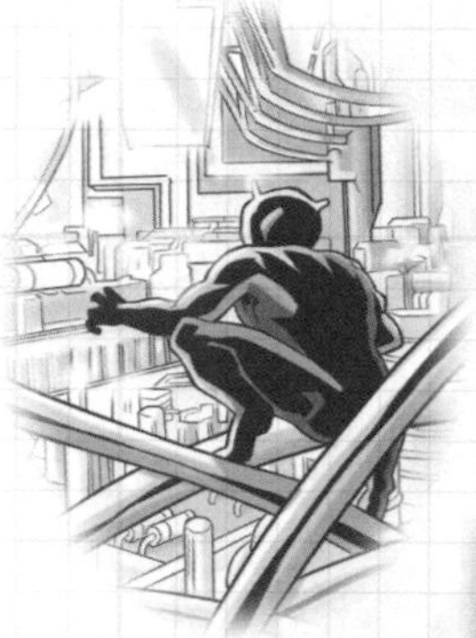

Ant-Man got super tiny, weaved his way in between the little lights on the billboards and hacked the main power grid—blasting the Frost Giants with **161 MEGAWATTS** of power.

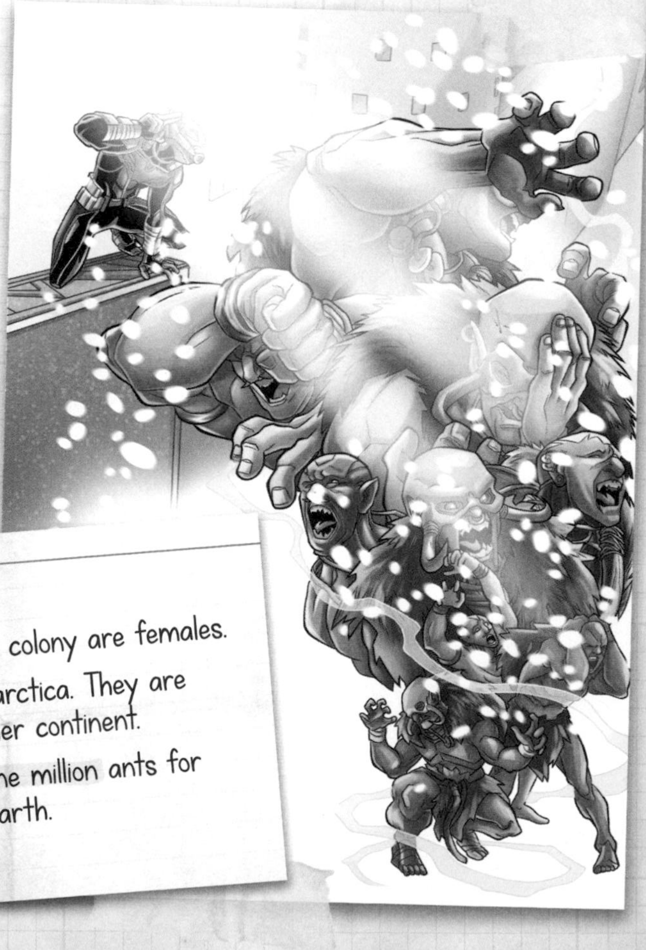

The blinding lights were so hot, the frosty foes began to melt away!

REAL ANT FACTS

- Almost all ants in a colony are females.
- No ants live in Antarctica. They are found on every other continent.
- There are about one million ants for every human on earth.

Just then, Ant-Man received word that the Avengers had vanquished Thanos. That meant it was time to send Loki packing, too. I snatched the Cosmic Cube and with it blasted Loki to infinity and beyond.

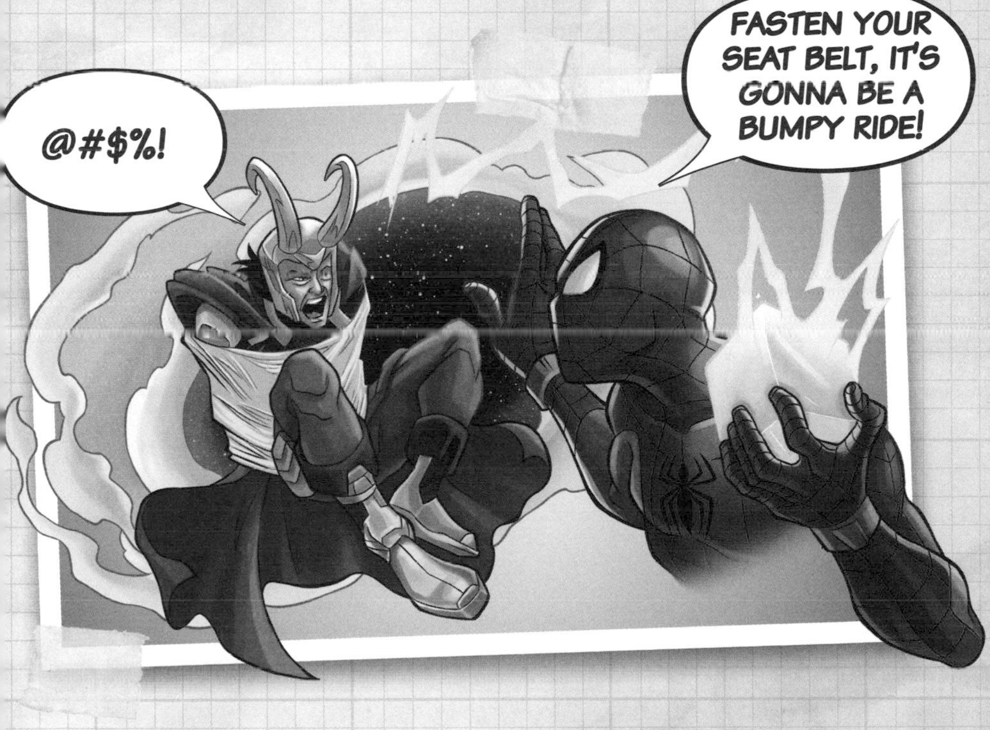
@#$%!
FASTEN YOUR SEAT BELT, IT'S GONNA BE A BUMPY RIDE!

He thanked me by screaming nasty things that I won't repeat because Aunt May taught me not to use **that kind of language.**

TIMES SQUARE SCARE!

IS MASKED MENACE MASTERMIND IN MIDTOWN MELTDOWN?

COVER STORY BY J. JONAH JAMESON

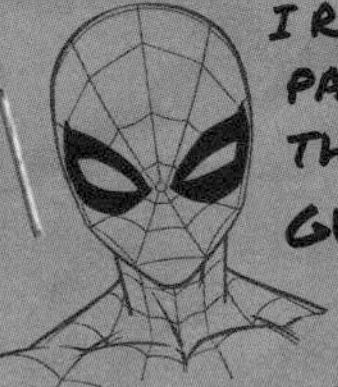

I RISK MY LIFE TO SNAP A FANTASTIC FRONT PAGE PHOTO WHILE SAVING THE CITY, AND THIS IS THE THANKS I GET FROM MY BOSS. GUESS THE "J" STANDS FOR JERK.

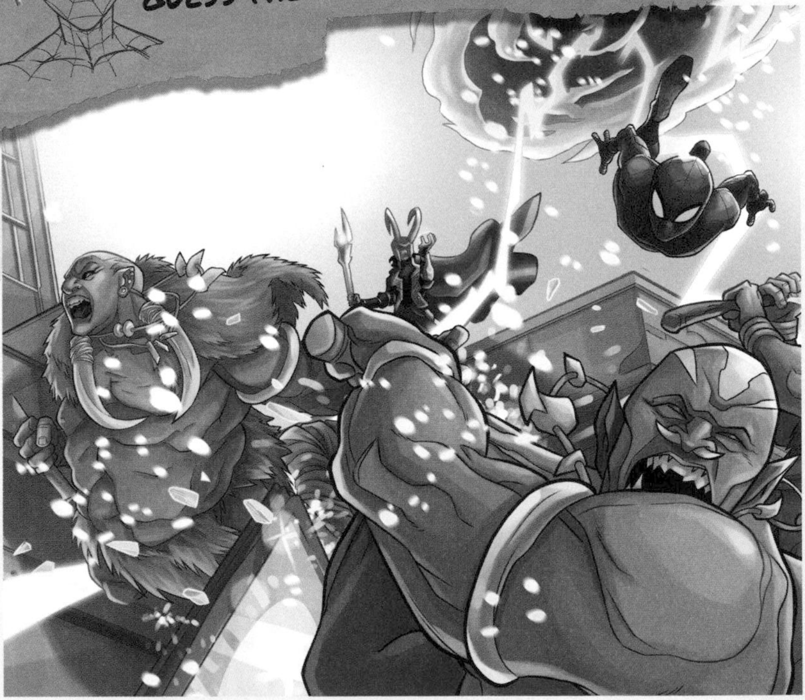

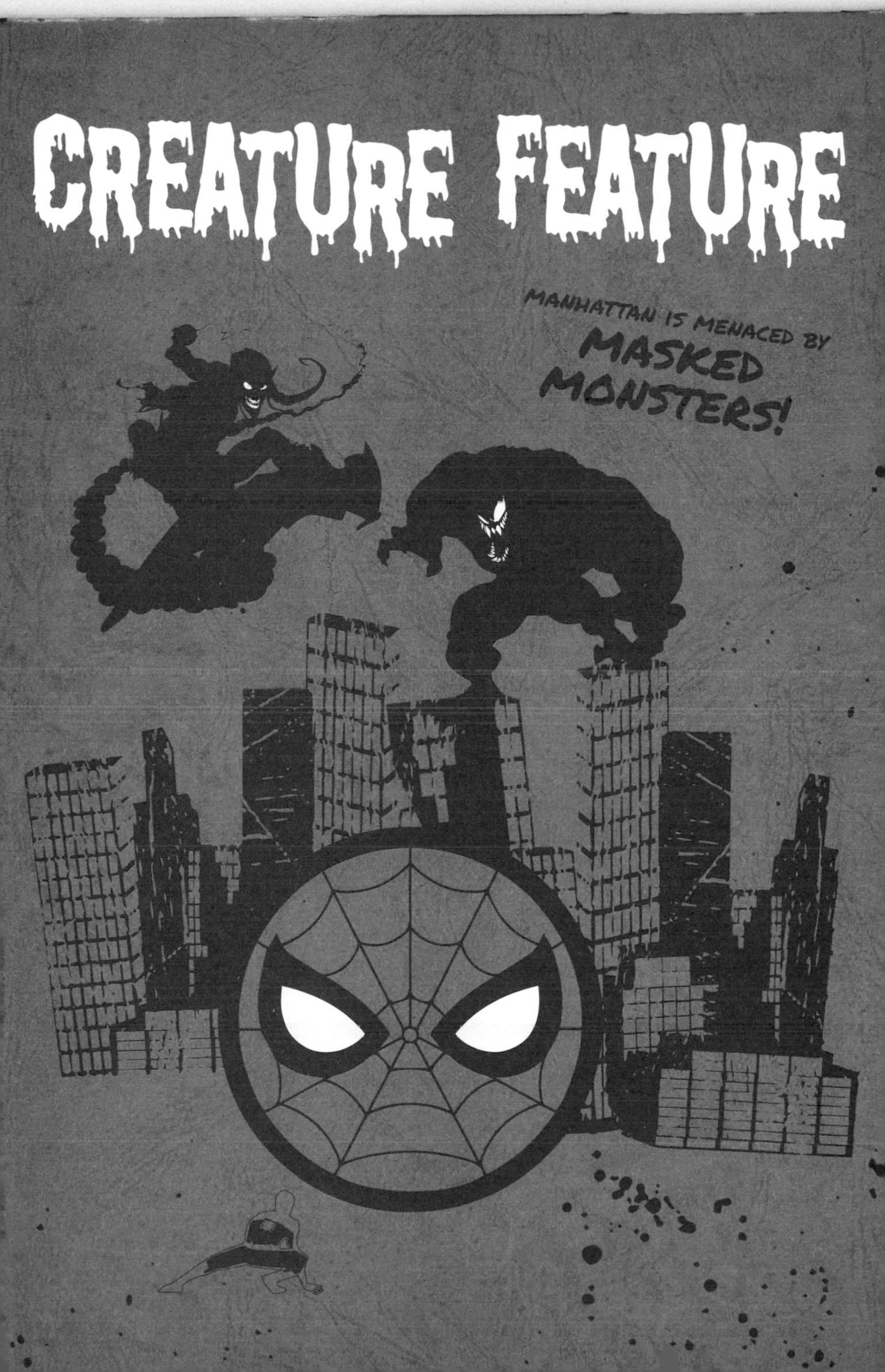
CREATURE FEATURE
MANHATTAN IS MENACED BY
MASKED
MONSTERS!

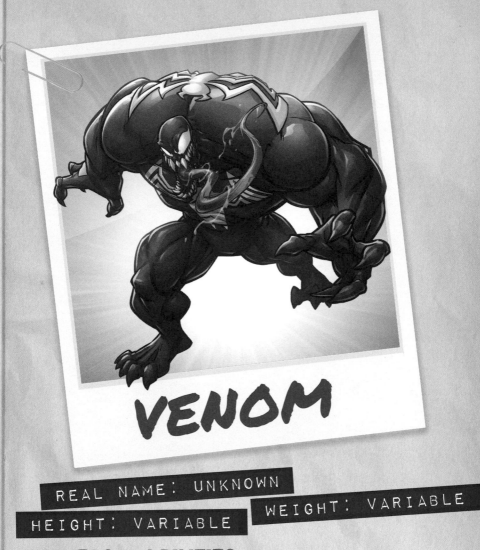

VENOM

REAL NAME: UNKNOWN

HEIGHT: VARIABLE

WEIGHT: VARIABLE

POWERS & ABILITIES

- THE SYMBIOTE GRANTS SUPER-STRENGTH, AGILITY, AND DURABILITY
- CAN EXUDE TENDRILS AND PRODUCE A WEB-LIKE FLUID OF ITS OWN SUBSTANCE
- HAS THE ABILITY TO MIMIC CLOTHING AND CAMOUFLAGE ITSELF
- THE SYMBIOTE IS WEAKENED BY HIGH DECIBELS OF SOUND AND EXTREME HEAT

Venom is the kind of creature that will make your skin crawl...**LITERALLY.** An amorphous entity, this symbiotic being has the reverse attributes of a parasite. It will take on the same shape as its host body, coating it like a costume, and enhance it exponentially. The symbiote feeds off of the anger and negative energy of its wearer, thus transforming itself into the massive, menacing manifestation of malice known as **VENOM!**

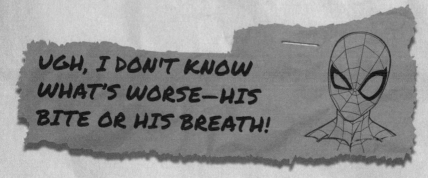

UGH, I DON'T KNOW WHAT'S WORSE—HIS BITE OR HIS BREATH!

GREEN GOBLIN

REAL NAME: NORMAN OSBORN

HEIGHT: 5'11"

WEIGHT: 185 LBS.

POWERS & ABILITIES

- SUPERHUMAN STRENGTH AND DURABILITY

- HIGH-SPEED GLIDER EQUIPPED WITH HIGH-TECH ARMAMENTS

- WEAPONS INCLUDE PUMPKIN BOMBS AND RAZOR-SHARP
  BATWING PROJECTILES

- GLOVES ARE CAPABLE OF DISCHARGING
  POWERFUL ELECTRIC BLASTS

Once a successful businessman and industrialist, Norman Osborn was left mentally deranged after—guess what—a lab accident in which he was testing an experimental serum. Now he uses his vast wealth, genius intellect, and advanced knowledge in engineering and chemistry to plague the people of the city as the **GREEN GOBLIN!**

(Dude, all that time and effort and you could've crushed it as a cosplayer at the New York Comic-Con instead of being an evil super villain.)

Just sayin'...

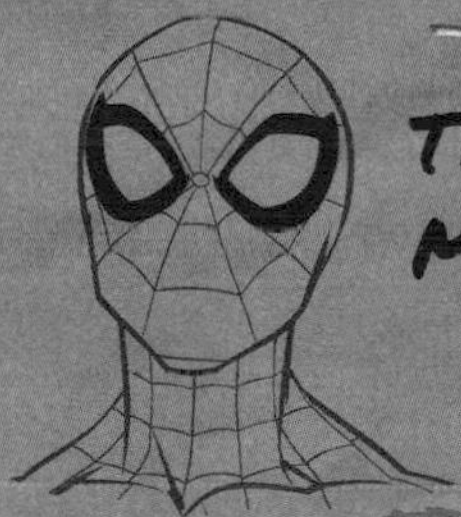

THIS GREEN GHOUL IS MORE TRICKS THAN TREATS!

Journal Entry 15:

This morning I rushed straight to the Daily Bugle, and surprised myself by making it in on time. I was hoping I wouldn't have to hear my boss yelling at me. No dice. He still yelled. But this time it was to tell me that the Lizard was on the loose and that it was my job to get him a front-page photo.

No matter what.

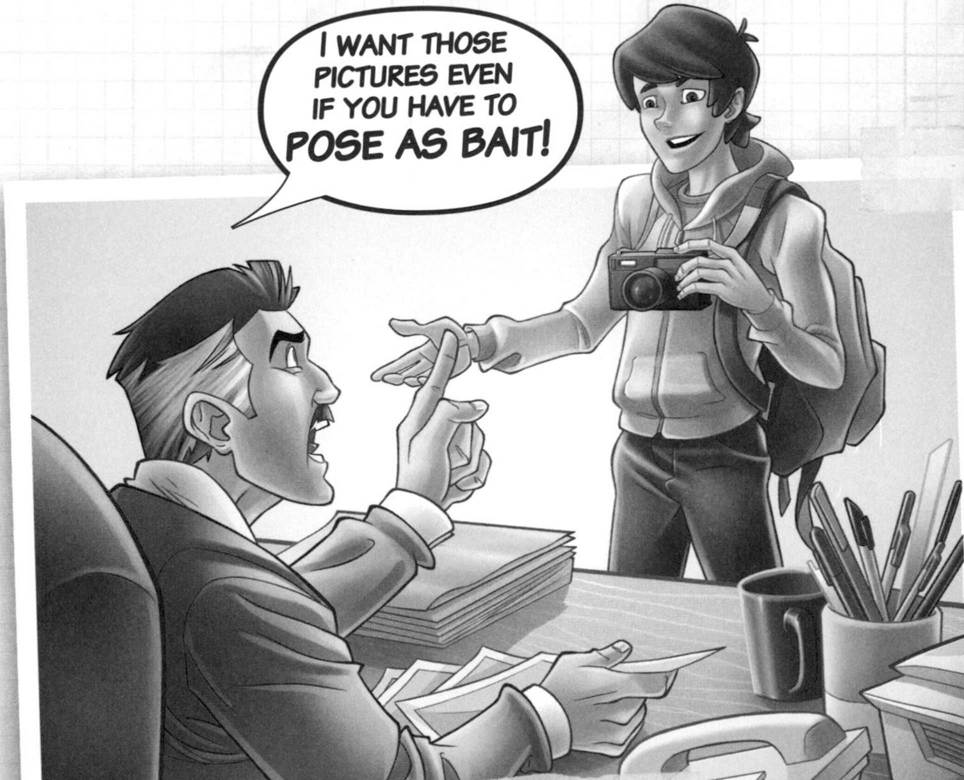
I WANT THOSE PICTURES EVEN IF YOU HAVE TO POSE AS BAIT!

Getting J.J. those pictures may have been Peter Parker's job, but it was Spider-Man's job to keep the city safe from the Lizard. And if the Lizard was on the loose, that meant that his alter ego, Dr. Connors, was in trouble. When the doc changes into that scaly scoundrel, he's a danger to himself as well.

All I had to do to find him was follow the police sirens and the trail of wreckage. That was the easy part. Then came the hard part: luring him back to his lab so I could administer the antidote.

Guess I was going to be bait after all!

LOOK AT ME!
I'M A YUMMY SPIDEY SNACK!

Lizard took the bait like a radioactive spider with an appetite for a teenage science geek...and tried to take a bite! I bobbed up the streets. I weaved down the avenues. The Lizard was catching up and my Spider-Sense tingled each time the rampaging reptile snapped those **GIANT CHOMPERS** at me.

Ultimately, J.J.'s misguided advice worked to my advantage, as I was able to lead the Lizard back into the lab. And since the doc had all his vials clearly marked I found the antidote in no time. Presto! Change-O!

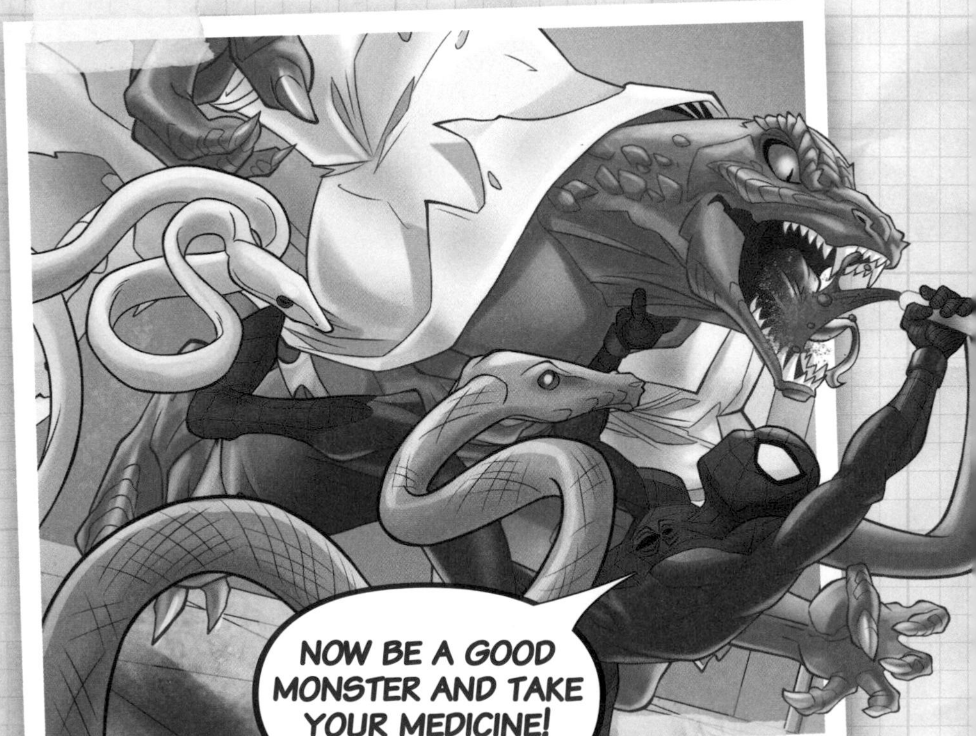
NOW BE A GOOD MONSTER AND TAKE YOUR MEDICINE!

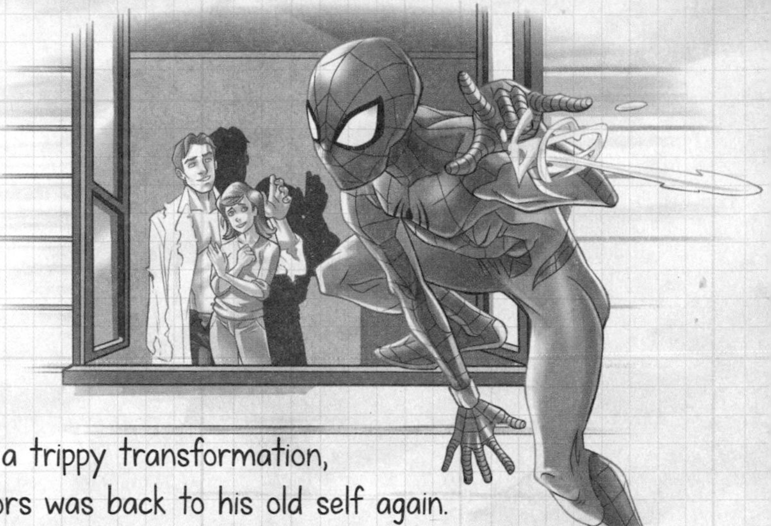

After a trippy transformation, Dr. Connors was back to his old self again. He and his wife Martha were happy to have things back to normal, and they thanked me profusely for my help. I wanted to stick around and learn more about the doc's research, but I was on the clock.

Later that afternoon, I brought J.J. his front-page photo. The cranky old curmudgeon was thrilled. Seeing him smile made me feel like I was face to face with the Lizard all over again!

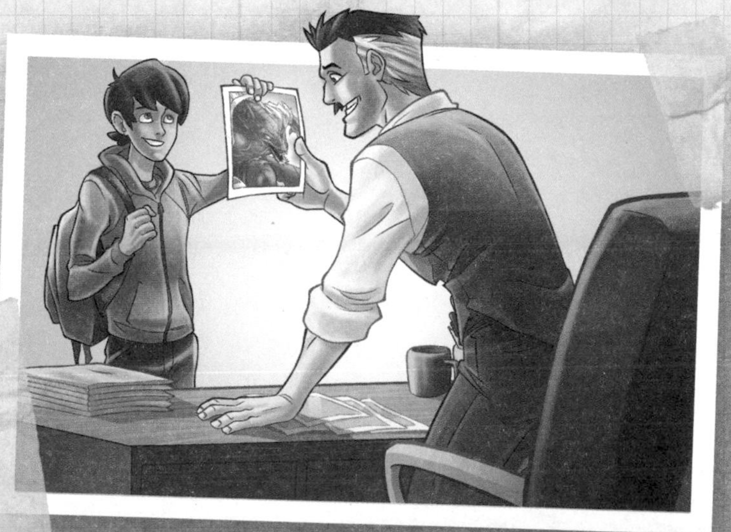

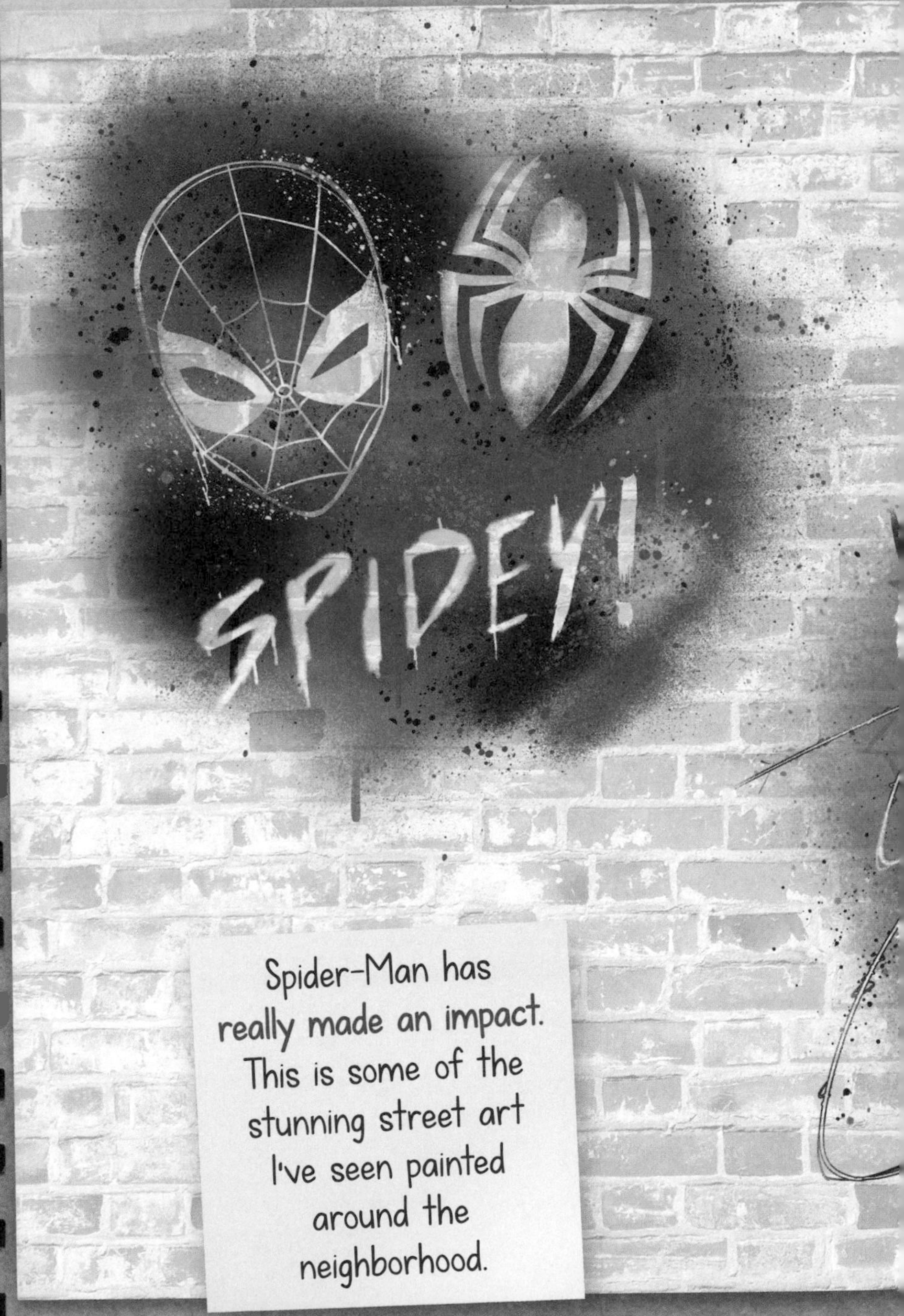
SPIDEY!

Spider-Man has really made an impact. This is some of the stunning street art I've seen painted around the neighborhood.

It's a great and humbling honor to have your portrait done by such talented artists.

(NOW I KNOW WHY THE MONA LISA IS ALWAYS SMILING!)

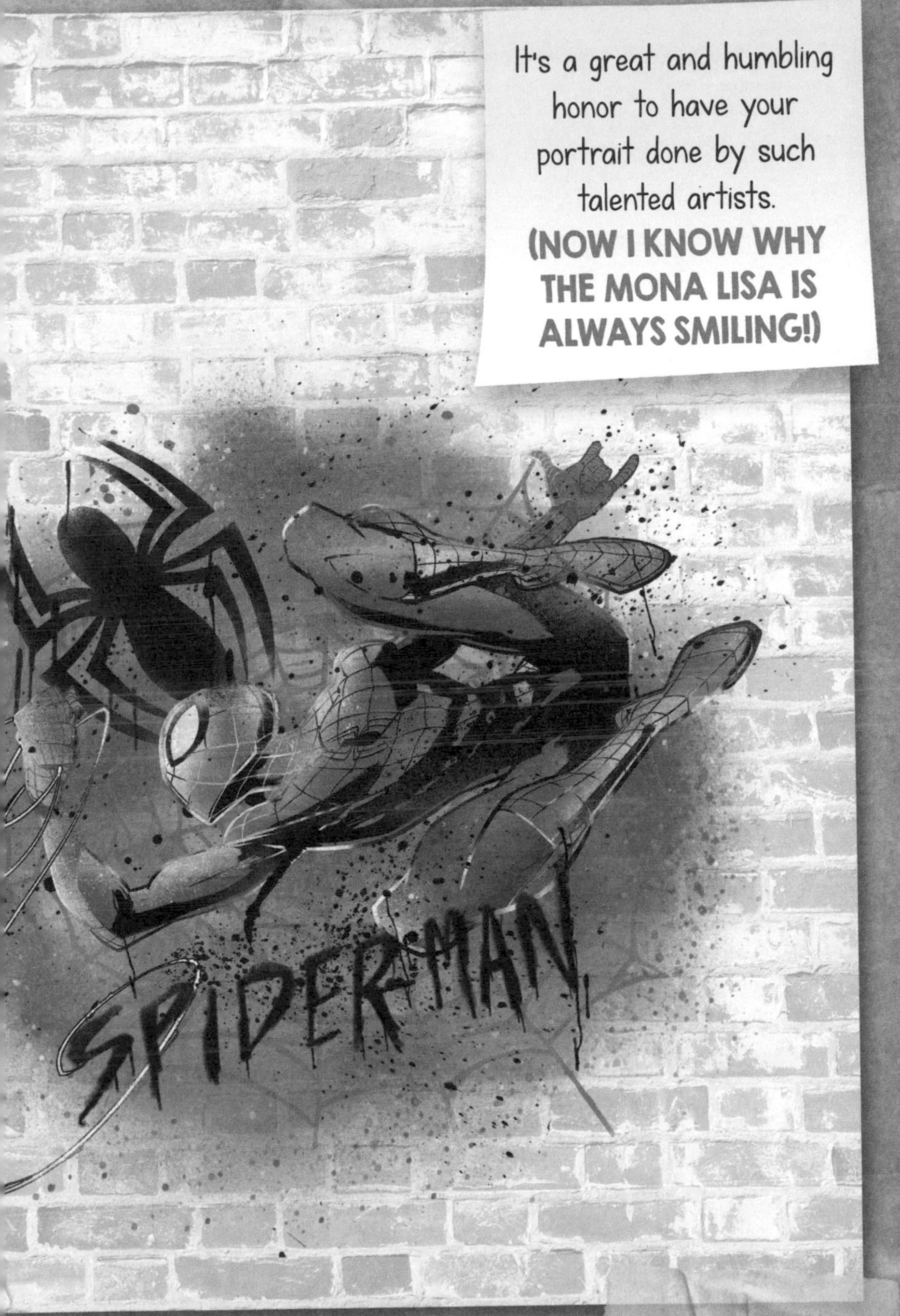
SPIDER-MAN

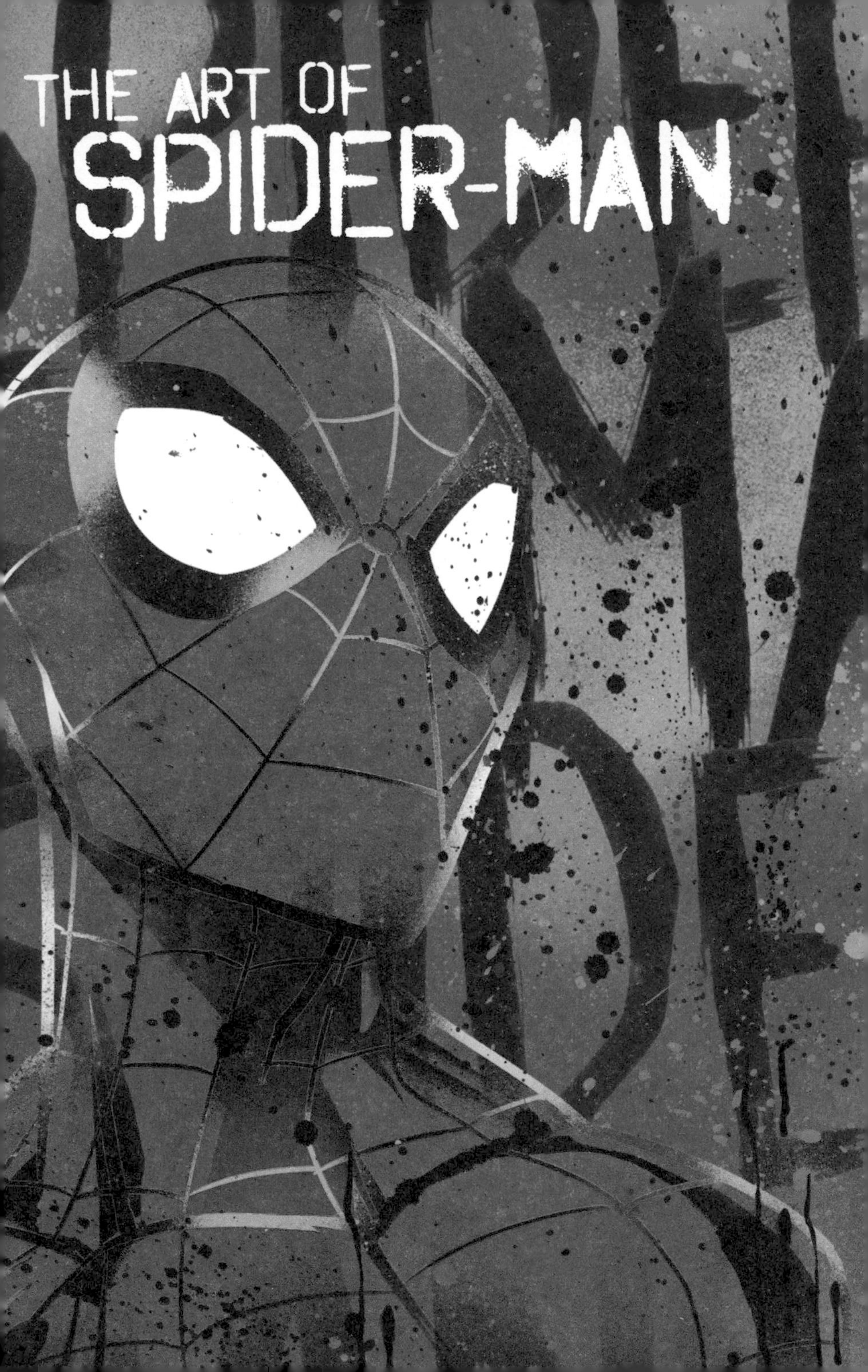
THE ART OF
SPIDER-MAN

JOURNAL ENTRY 16:

After an exhausting week of schoolwork, today I finally got to sleep in. The sweet smell of Aunt May's chocolate chip pancakes wafted through the air. I jumped out of bed faster than Spider-Man dodging one of Doc Ock's mechanical arms and raced downstairs. This was shaping up to be the perfect Saturday!

BREAKFAST IS THE MOST IMPORTANT MEAL OF THE DAY!

Suddenly, my phone started buzzing. It was J.J. and he was about to blow. I forgot that I had work! Scarfing down my pancakes, I kissed Aunt May goodbye and rushed out. I needed to get to the Daily Bugle fast, so I changed into Spider-Man. This way, I'd be getting there just before J.J. exploded.

As soon as I reached the Bugle, my Spider-Sense tingled. Smoke was billowing out of Jameson's office!

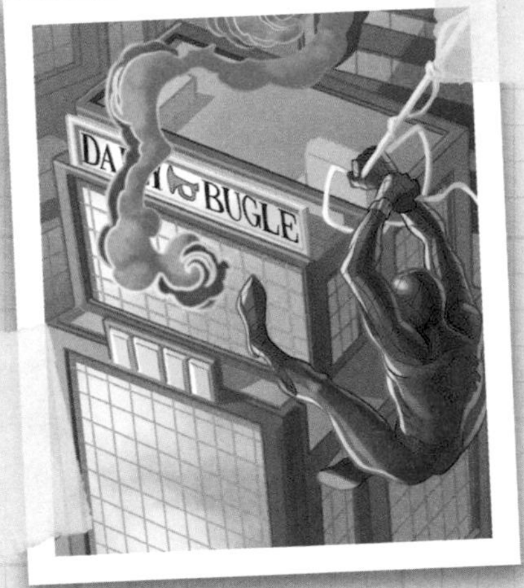
BUGLE

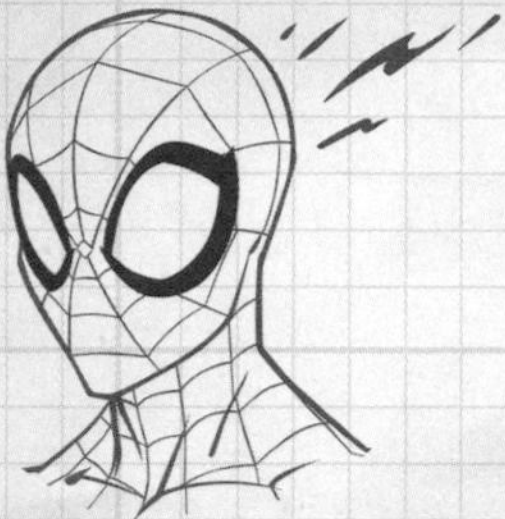

Guess I spoke too soon!

Swinging downward, I discovered an old foe was up to new tricks—**MYSTERIO!** After his show business career went up in smoke, Mysterio turned to a life of crime. Now, the maniacal master of illusion was demanding that the paper print positive press to boost his brand...**OR ELSE!**

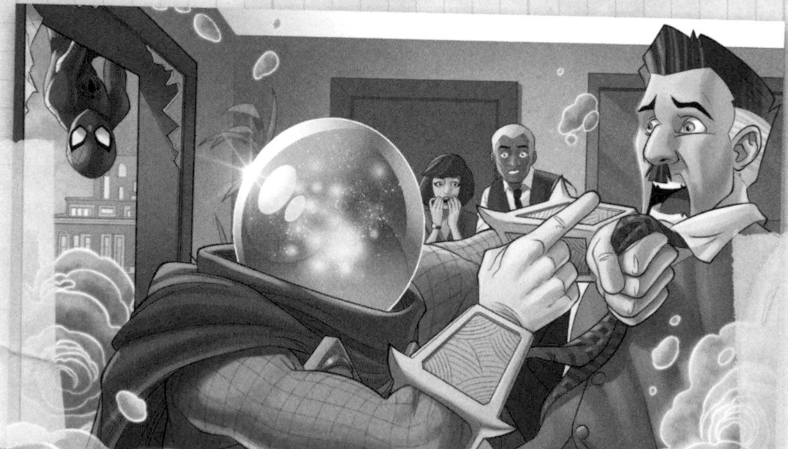

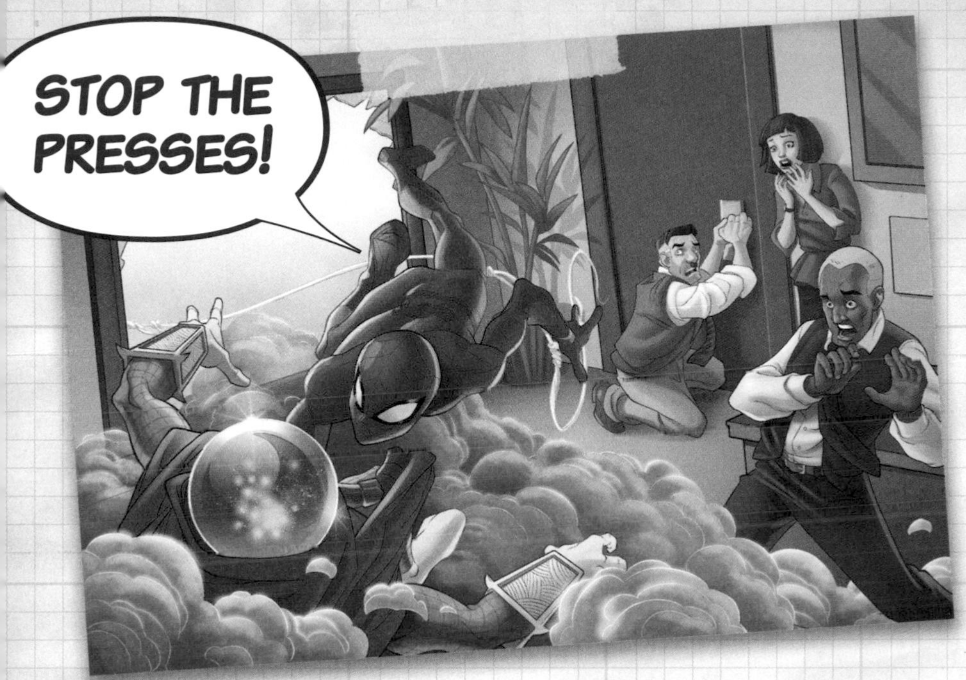
STOP THE PRESSES!

It was Spider-Man's turn to steal the spotlight. This distraction was just what I needed to give J.J. and my coworkers, Betty Brant and Robbie Robertson, a chance to escape.

Which was good for them, but bad for me.

Mysterio reached into his bag of tricks and released a potent cloud of hallucinogenic gas.

Mysterio's mist quickly filled the air. My mask filtered out most of the terrible toxin, but I still got a bit of a brain drain. As soon as the ill-tempered illusionist removed that fish bowl of a helmet, I lost my mind. There, standing a few feet away from me was... **MYSELF!?**

Logically, I knew this was all a trick. But emotionally...it was a different story. An overwhelming rush of guilt and anxiety washed over me. It felt like all my insecurities manifested in this hyper-real hallucination. I was momentarily stunned by the shock and paralyzed in place.

Mysterio took advantage of this opportunity and sucker punched me.

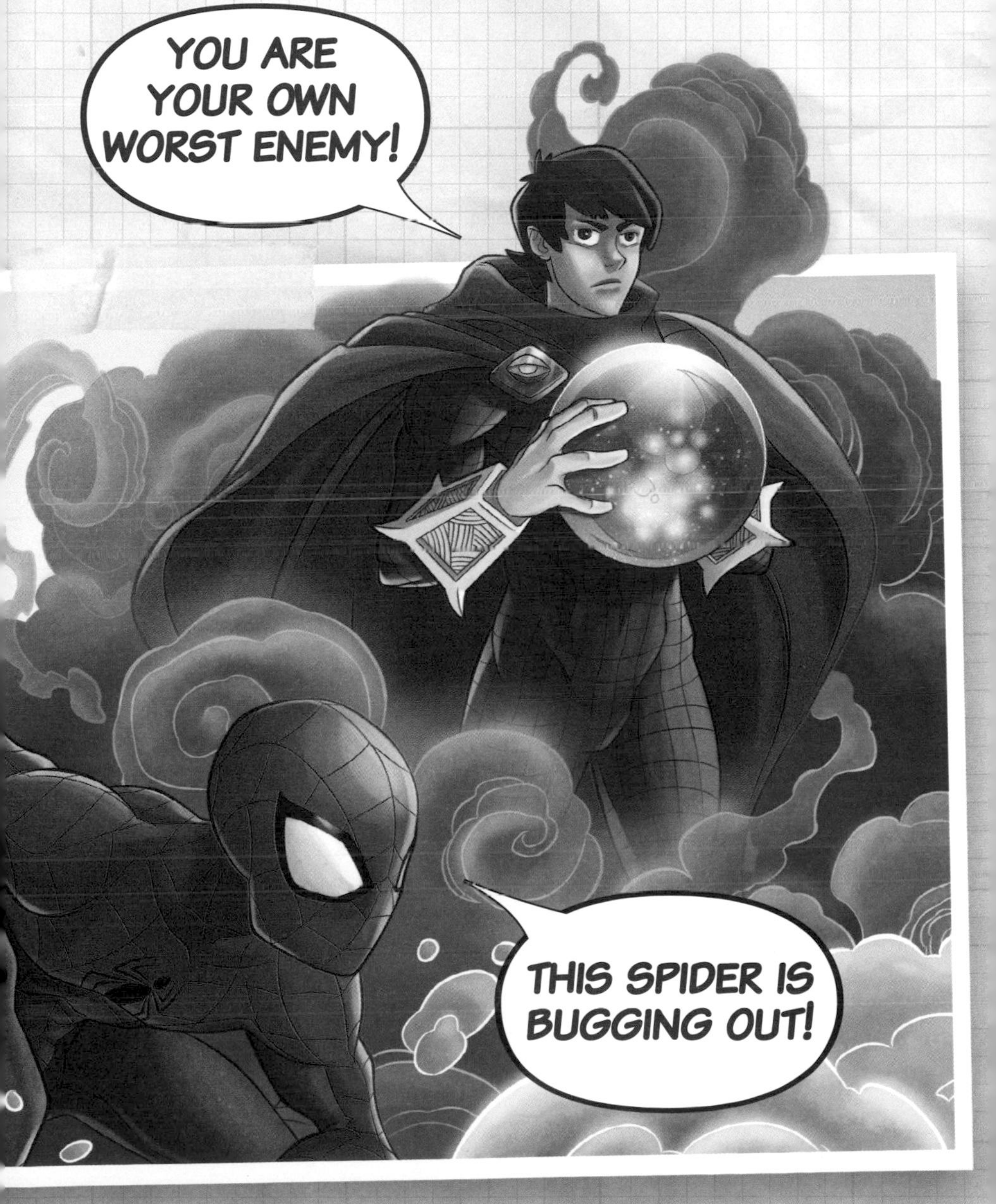
YOU ARE YOUR OWN WORST ENEMY!
THIS SPIDER IS BUGGING OUT!

Ironically, Mysterio's sucker punch was just what I needed to reboot my hard drive. Now it was time to return the favor and give him a hard shut down.

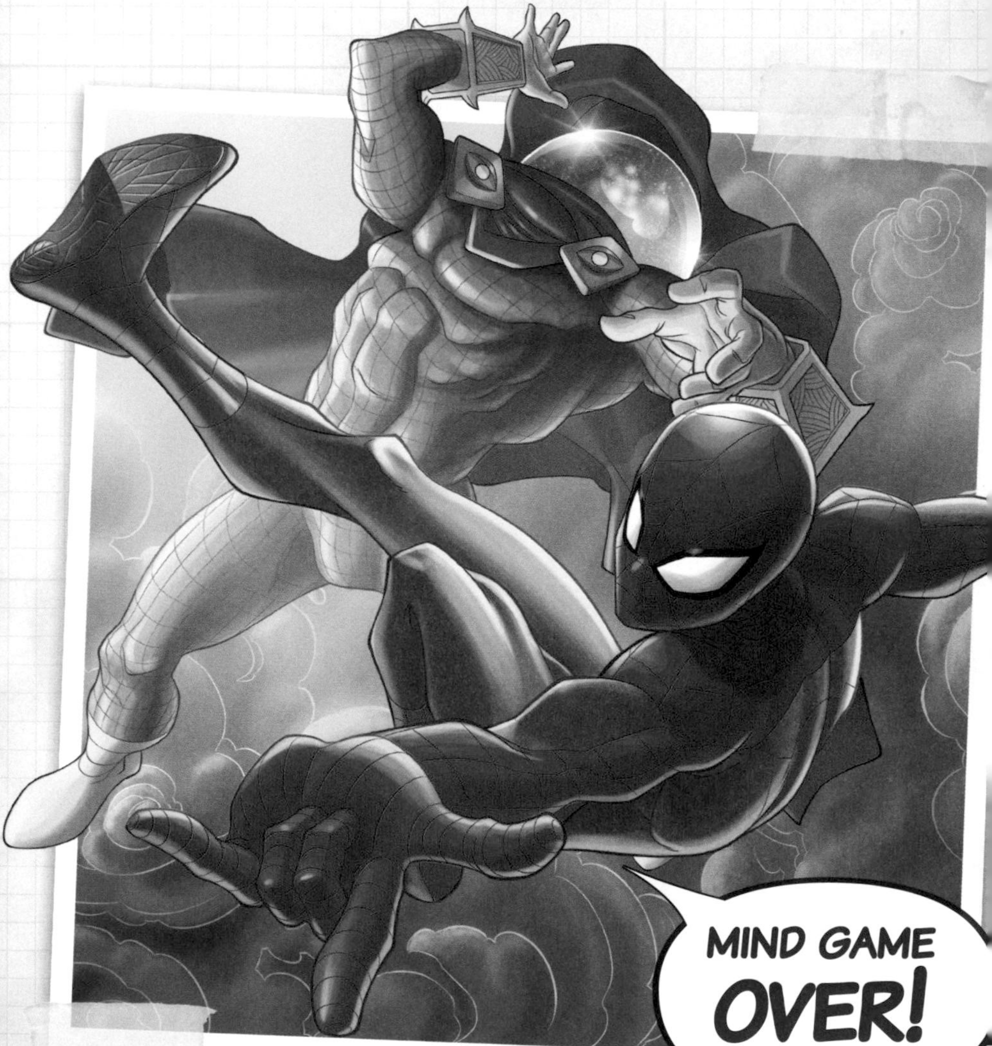
MIND GAME OVER!

With Mysterio down for the count, I changed into my civilian clothes seconds before the police arrived.

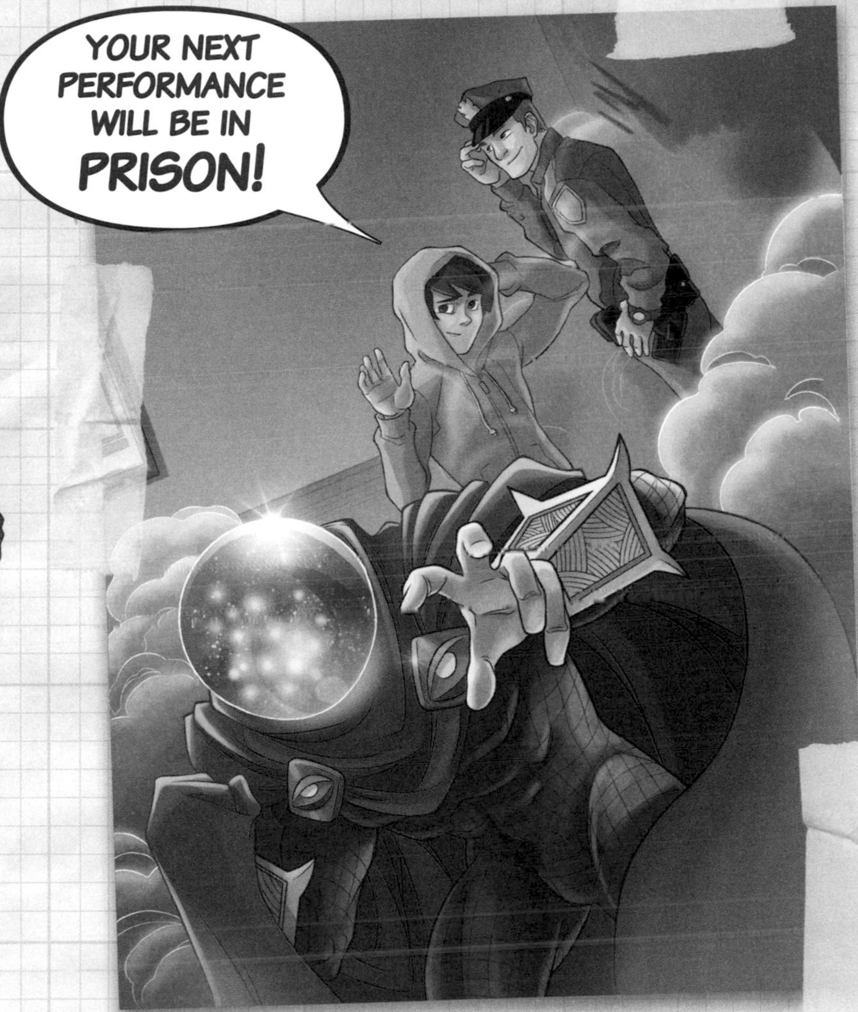
YOUR NEXT PERFORMANCE WILL BE IN PRISON!

While carting off the criminal, a kind cop named Officer Merkel informed me that Betty and Robbie were safe and that Jameson had taken the rest of the day off. I bet he went home to change his pants!

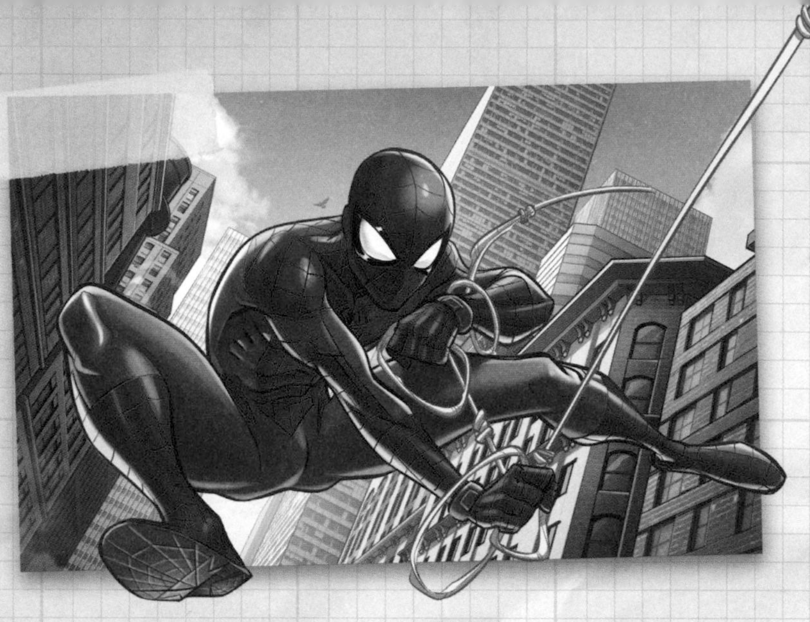

Journal Entry 17:

After what felt like weeks, I **FINALLY** got my day off. No school, no work, no bad guys to battle. Just the breeze in my face as I cruised up Fifth Avenue in style. Honestly, is there any other way to travel?

But suddenly, my Spider-Sense tingled...but it was a good tingle. Up ahead, at the Avengers Tower, a ravishing redhead caught my eye. It was the team's resident super-spy, **BLACK WIDOW!**

She hailed me like a cab and told me I was just in time for the Avengers' annual picnic. Apparently they had tried calling me and got no answer.

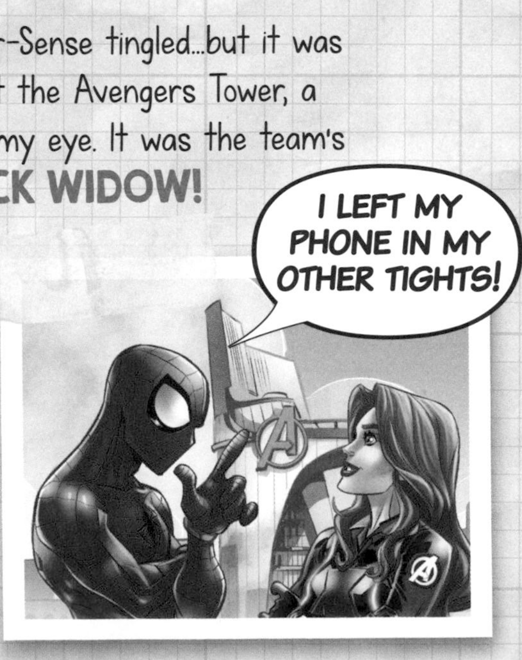
I LEFT MY PHONE IN MY OTHER TIGHTS!

The mere concept boggled my mind. **ME?** Invited to the Avengers' picnic? I was floating on air. And pretty soon I was swinging through it with Black Widow herself hitching a ride to Central Park.

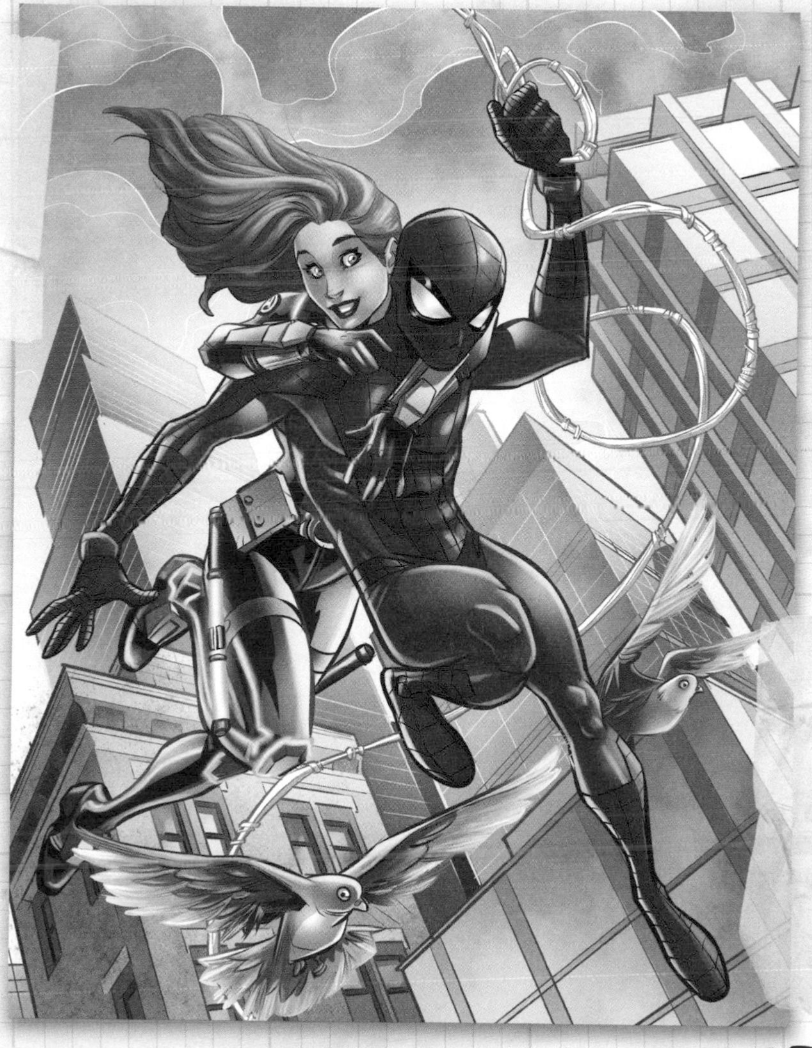

IS THIS REAL LIFE??

I'd never been to a super hero picnic before, so I had no idea what to expect. It was basically like any other picnic in the park: good friends, good food, and fun games. No big deal.

However, unlike any other picnic in the park, this one also had **IRON MAN, HULK, NICK FURY, THOR, HAWKEYE, BLACK WIDOW, CAPTAIN AMERICA, ANT-MAN,** and a few of my close personal powerful pals.

They even made a Mysterio-shaped piñata in my honor.

I HAD DIED AND GONE TO SUPER HERO HEAVEN.

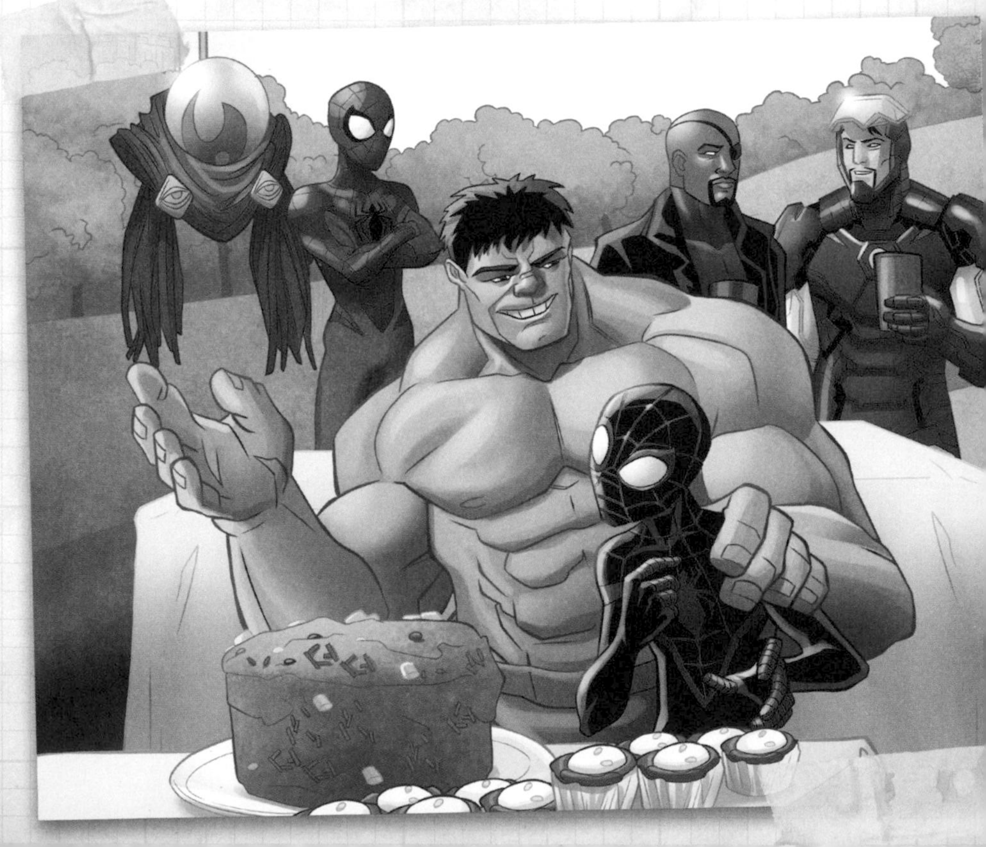

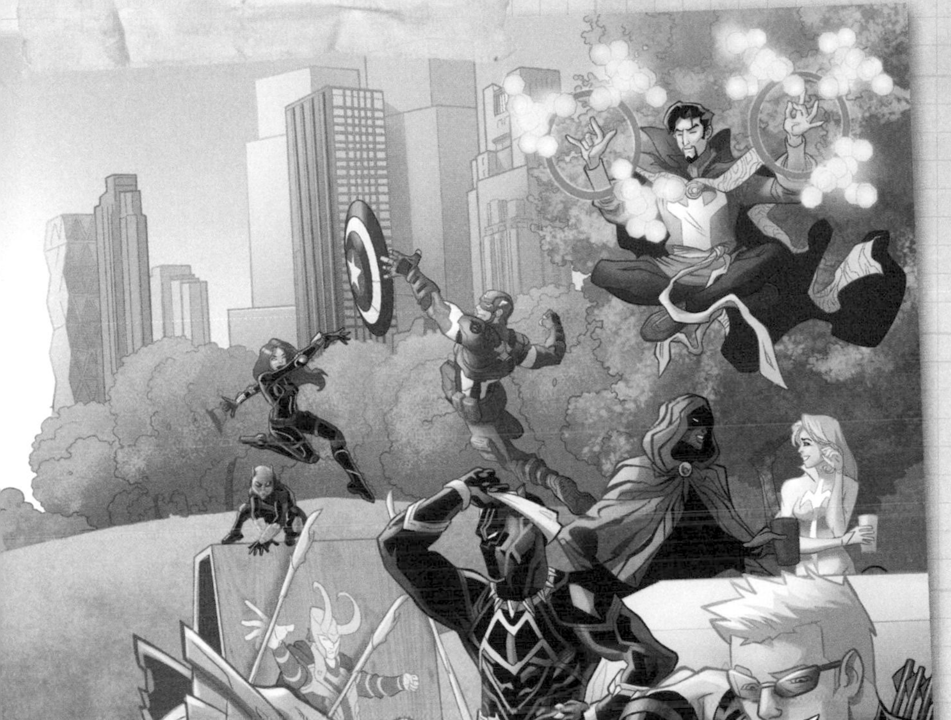

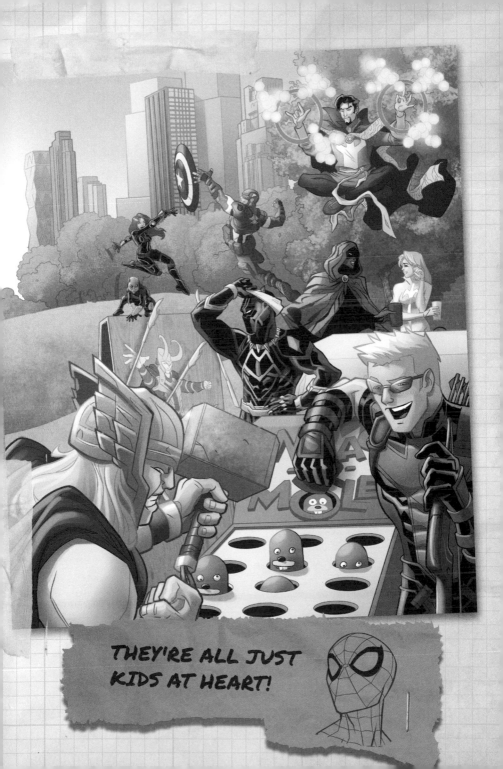

THEY'RE ALL JUST KIDS AT HEART!

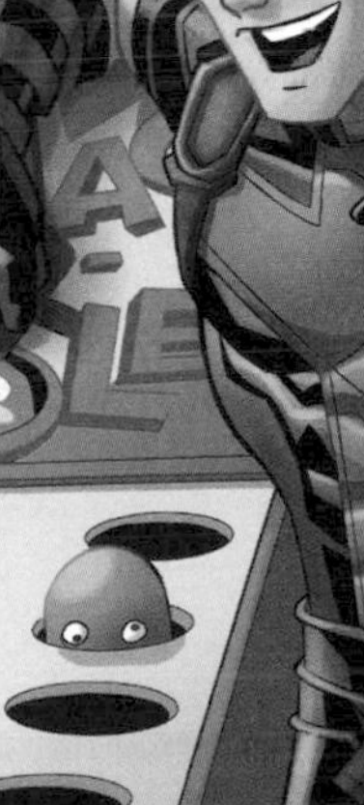

They say a picture is worth a thousand words, but this one is worth all the words I know and all the words I don't know.

In **EVERY** language.

I have finally found my place in the world... and it is right alongside Earth's Mightiest Heroes!

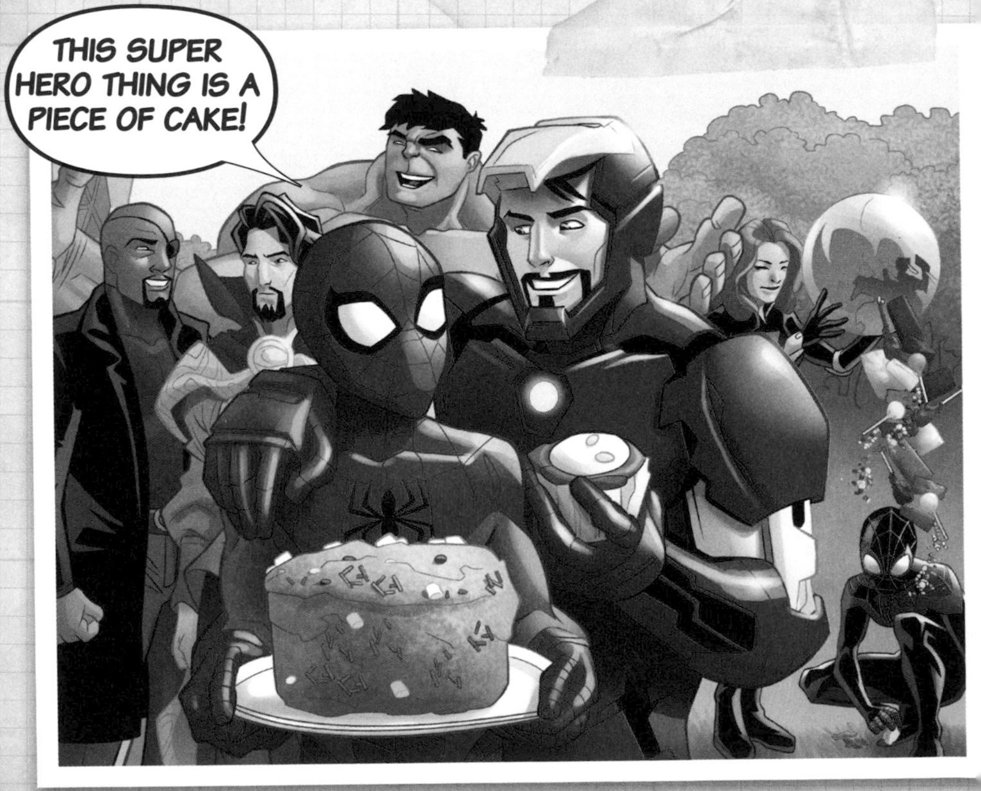
THIS SUPER HERO THING IS A PIECE OF CAKE!

SPIDER-MAN: WEBBED WONDER

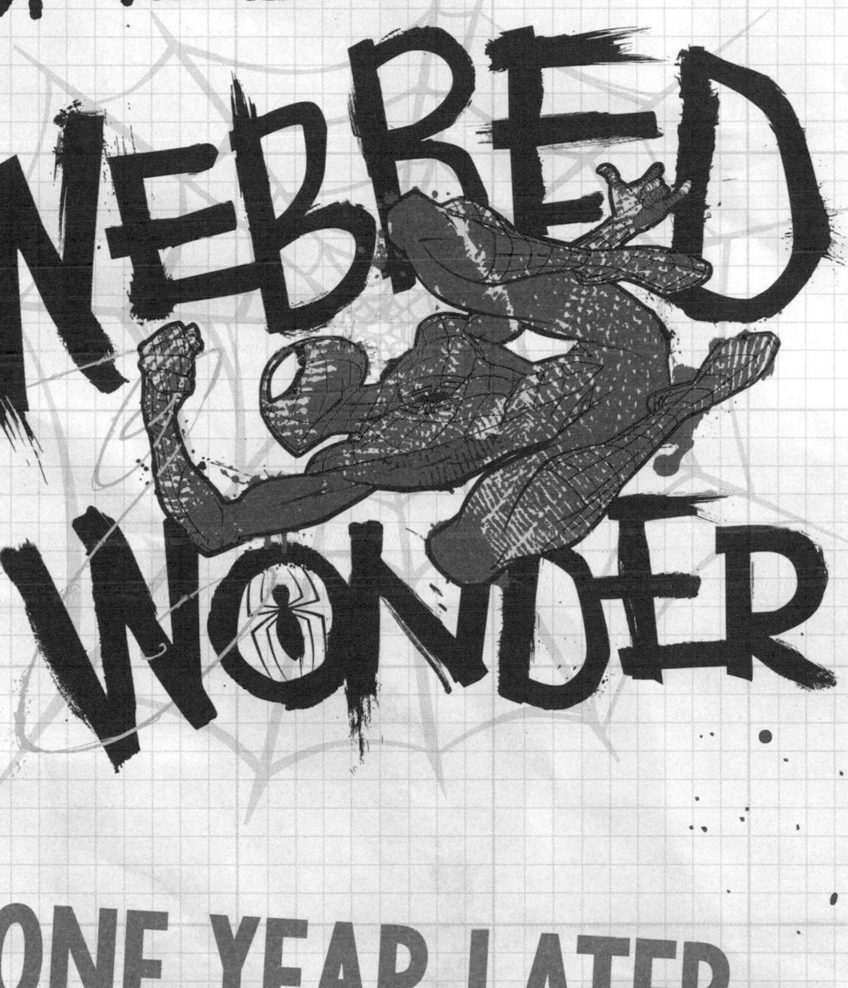

ONE YEAR LATER...

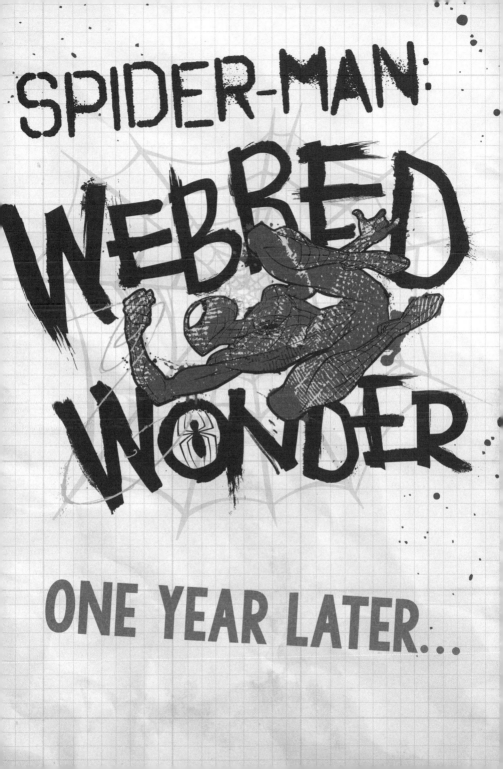

Wow. I can't believe a year has come and gone. It feels like that radioactive spider bit me just yesterday. Today, while I was cleaning out my room, I came across the proto-suit—my first attempt at creating Spider-Man's "look"—and I have to say that I've really come a **LOOOONG** way since then!

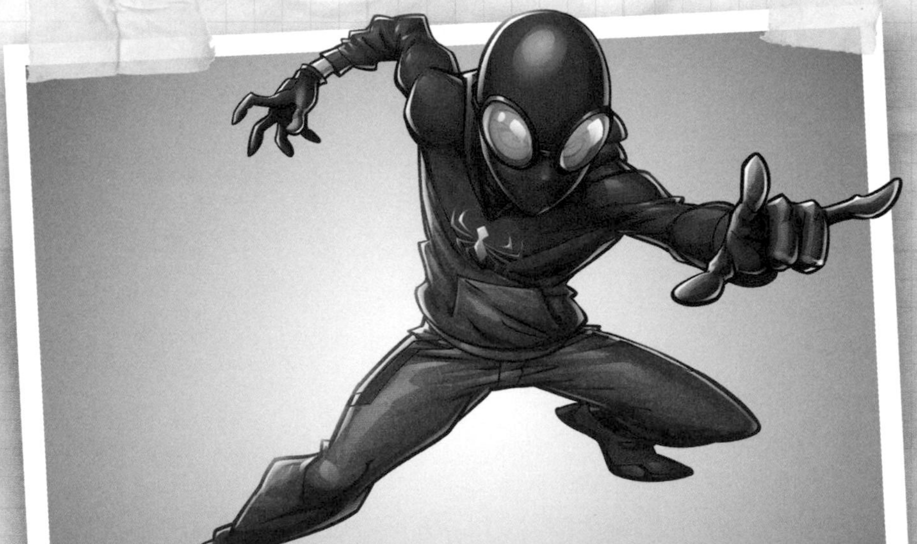
BEFORE

AFTER

Looking back at all of this stuff is bittersweet. The birth of one hero was caused by the death of another. There would be no present-day Spider-Man without the loss of Uncle Ben.

I miss him every day. And each day I do my best to make the world a better, safer place in his honor.

Ben Parker believed that I would go on to do great things.

I like to think that I made him proud.

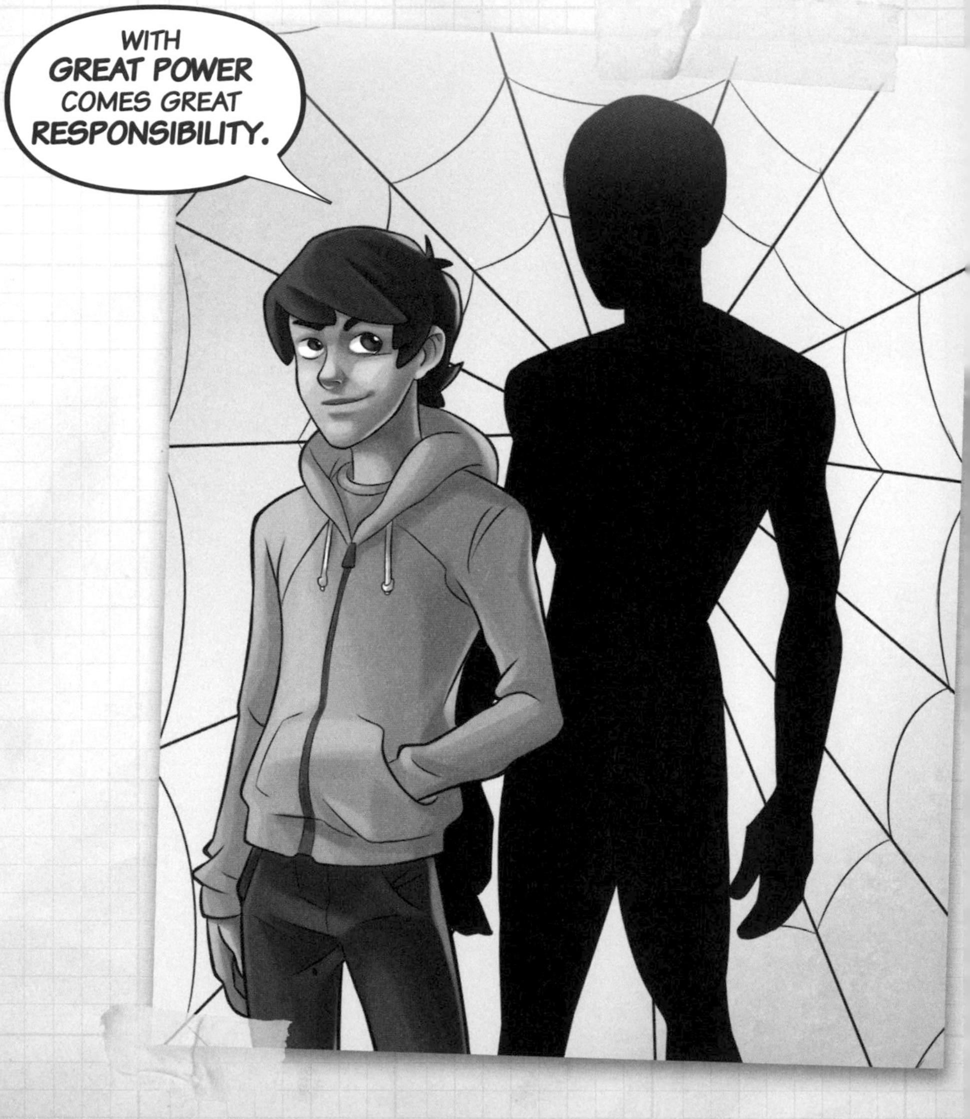
WITH GREAT POWER COMES GREAT RESPONSIBILITY.

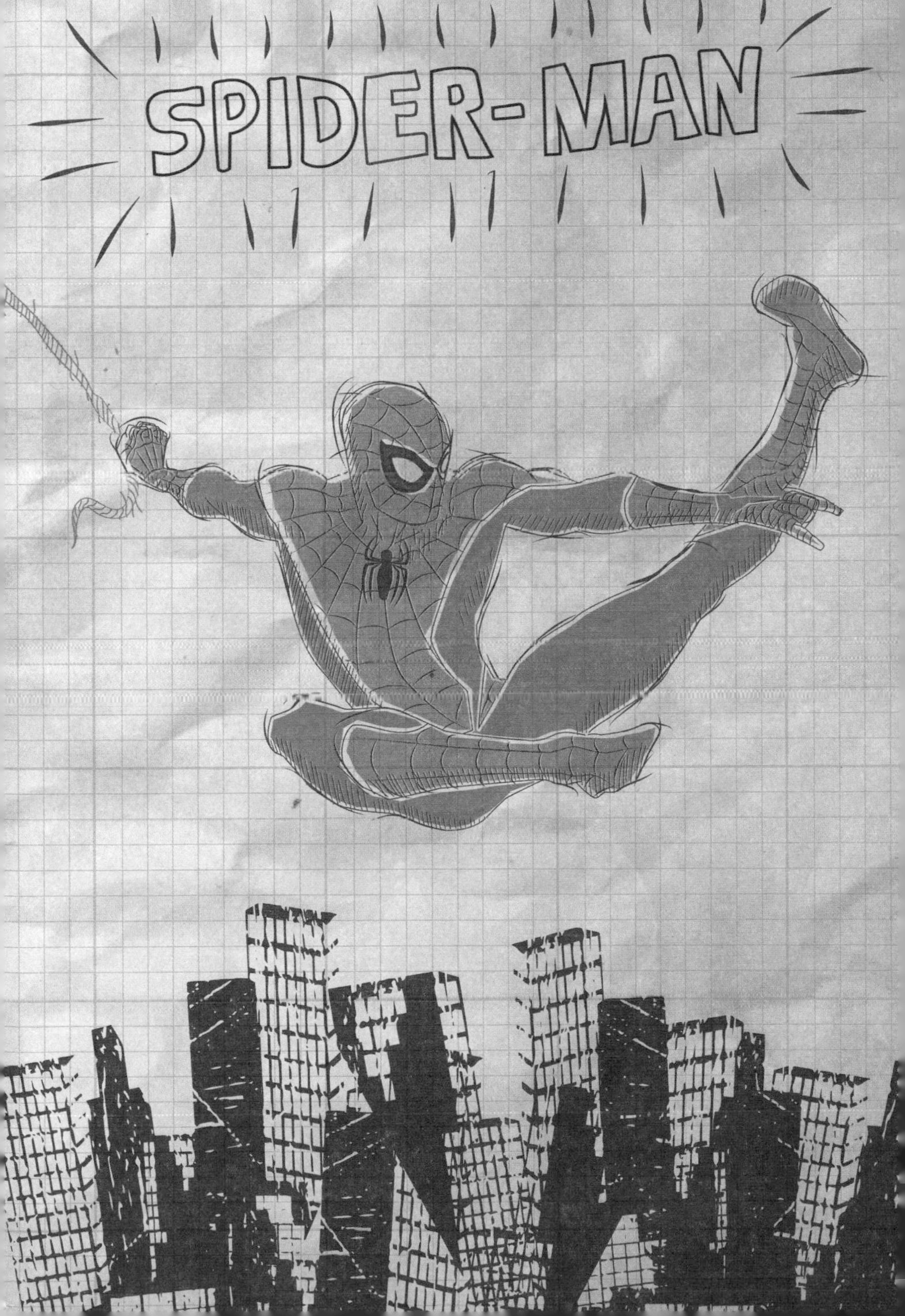
SPIDER-MAN

Studio Fun International
An imprint of Printers Row Publishing Group
A division of Readerlink Distribution Services, LLC
10350 Barnes Canyon Road, Suite 100, San Diego, CA 92121
www.studiofun.com

Written by John Sazaklis
Illustrated by Simone Buonfantino, Roberto DiSalvo, and Aurelio Mazzara
Illustrations painted by Tommaso Moscardin, Ekaterina Myshalova, and Davide Mastrolonardo
Designed by Shaun Doniger

Studio Fun International is a registered trademark of Readerlink Distribution Services, LLC.
All notations of errors or omissions should be addressed to Studio Fun International,
Editorial Department, at the above address.

ISBN: 978-0-7944-3964-4
Manufactured, printed, and assembled in Stevens Point, Wisconsin, United States of America.
First printing, June 2017. 6/17/WOR
21 20 19 18 17 1 2 3 4 5